PRAISE FOR MILES FROM MOTOWN

"*Miles from Motown* is a beautiful coming-of-age story. The prose-poetry fits perfectly like a well-worn baseball glove. Exhilarating. Inspiring. I couldn't put it down!"

— Ronit Bezalel, award-winning director of *Seventy Acres in Chicago: Cabrini Green*

"Like the city it's named for, this novel has an engine all its own and that engine never stops. Once you start reading, you can't put it down. It's more than a book, it's a whole experience; a full-throttle reminder of how it feels to come of age in a chaotic time and place. Georgia's journey speaks to the poet in all of us."

— J.S. Puller, author of *Captain Superlative*

MILES FROM MOTOWN

Lisa Sukenic

Fitzroy Books

Published by Fitzroy Books
An imprint of
Regal House Publishing, LLC
Raleigh, NC 27612
All rights reserved

https://fitzroybooks.com

Printed in the United States of America

ISBN -13 (paperback): 9781646030644
ISBN -13 (epub): 9781646030897
Library of Congress Control Number: 2020941115

Interior and cover design by Lafayette & Greene
lafayetteandgreene.com
Cover images © by C.B. Royal

Regal House Publishing, LLC
https://regalhousepublishing.com

Printed in the United States of America

Dedicated with love to my parents,
Lawrence and Arlene Sukenic who grew up in Detroit,
May their memory be for a blessing

The last day of school

I can barely hear Mrs. Murphy
telling us to mail our poems for the city's
Spirit of Detroit Poetry Contest.
The classroom ceiling fan spins
round and round.
The whir isn't soft; it's a fast
twirling sound, like the cards that
Ceci and I put on our bike spokes.

She passes out envelopes,
to write our addresses.
I pause, pencil to envelope,
and take a breath,
hold the pencil tight, and write
Georgia Johnson,
1896 Winton, Detroit,
Aunt Birdie's address, not mine.

I start to sweat, not because I am on the third floor
on a hot day in the middle of June at
Rutherford Elementary School.
I know the rules, even though Mrs. Murphy
reads them aloud again.
"All poets must live in Detroit to win."
I am starting a lie,
but I don't care.

My parents are making us move
to the suburbs. I keep asking why, but
they won't tell me.

They are taking me too far from
who I know, too far to walk back here.
I want to stay stuck in time,
like a movie in slow motion.

Next year, my friends will go
to junior high in Detroit.
I won't be in class with my best friend, Ceci,
for the first time ever.
Mrs. Murphy says, "Gwendolyn Brooks will choose
the winning poem, and the winner will receive a letter in
    July."

Her words sound distant,
like they are moving through water.
"Remember how we read *Bronzeville, Boys and Girls* and
    learned to write like real poets?"
Mrs. Murphy places her hand on my shoulder,
"Especially you, Georgia."
I don't want to be called teacher's pet, so I barely look up.
"Don't forget to drop your entries in the mailbox."
She's telling us to have a
wonderful summer.
The word *wonderful*
and my life don't mix.

The worst part is that when my older brother, Ty,
comes back from Vietnam,
he will never live in
our old house again.

Last night at home

It is my last night here.
I'm awake, not wanting to go to sleep,
not wanting to go
tomorrow.
I write a poem instead.

On high

I remember
me flying in the air,
Ty's feet on my belly,
me balancing, steadying my arms
out to the side,
my large wingspan like a great blue heron.
I begin to lose my balance,
grab his strong hands.
That is what my
six-year-old self remembers.

The moving truck

I hear the high-pitched squeak of
brakes from the moving truck. I already said
my goodbyes to Ceci. She's left for Flint
to stay with her Grandma. I need to
give Aunt Birdie my goodbye hug.
She's gone back to her house to get something
for me, but I can't wait.

I follow her across the alley between our houses,
stones crunching beneath my feet
like quicksand, pulling me back.

I jump over a puddle
and reach the gate, remember the
tag games that my middle brother, Jerome,
and I played before he started acting
all teenage-like.

I look toward the alley,
grass growing between the two tire paths,
black-eyed Susan, dandelions,
and Queen Anne's Lace.

Aunt Birdie's skirt flies up,
the flower patterns waving,
like a sailboat caught in the wind.

I hug hard, burying my head on her shoulder.
I look up and she smiles with the same laugh lines Mama
    has.

"You go now… You're my brave girl. I'll see you soon."
I grab on tighter, don't want to lose this hugging feeling.
She hands me a change purse that jingles with coins.
It's lined with silky fabric. Inside she has left
her phone number and address.
Gently, she pulls my fingers off her skirt like
she did when I was young and I wanted to stay
at her house longer.

I'll try to pretend that the few miles
between here and there are small,
like an inch on a scale map and
I will be back to visit,
but it will never be the same.

Jerome and Daddy go first

It is four in the afternoon by the time the truck is loaded.
Jerome's friends from his baseball team have helped all day.
They have sweaty backs, shirts sticking to them.
They're giving each other pats and punches, and hugs
to Jerome and Daddy.
Daddy offers them each $10 bills that they refuse to take.
"Goodbye, Mr. Johnson," they all say.
Jerome stands on the other side of the street
and signals for him to back the truck out of the driveway.
I ride with Mama.

I can't look up or back, no time for tears now.
I promise myself to not wave or turn around
and become like Lot's wife in the Bible, who turned to salt,
but I can't help it.

We live at the end of the block near busy 7 Mile,
our block, my block.
I know the cracks in the sidewalk that always
catch our skates,
the tree that I was small enough to hide behind
for hide-and-seek,
Mr. Gregg listening to the Tigers game on the radio and
Weiss's Deli on our corner, just between our house and the
        alley.

We're now turning onto Greenfield.
There's the cleaners where I go get our ironed sheets,
Cunningham's drugstore, where Ceci and I pick
up super balls and the workers in smocks would slap our
        hands.
Two blocks down, the Kresge's Five & Dime, where we
get our Sanders hot fudge cream puffs
at the counter.

Mama turns onto the highway.
What was mine
and what I know
is gone.

Driving away

The ride seems long, even though it's only seven miles.
I read the signs along the John R. Highway.
I see the exit to Northland Mall, familiar
8 Mile Road, the viaduct, the dividing point,
my home gone and then unfamiliar,
and then I see a "Welcome to Southfield" sign.

I feel something in my pocket.
It's the tree manual card that I read to Daddy
when he dug up our oak tree.
My eyes blur. I barely see Step 4.
"If the taproot is damaged, it will not survive."
Taproot, taproot, taproot, tap my foot, tap, tap.
"Georgia! Stop, please!"
"Mama, please go back home."
Mama just turns and gives me her *no* look.

Subdivided

Highway ends and slides into the
new subdivision,
houses under construction,
skeletons with new 2 x 4 planks,
empty rooms and stairways reaching to nowhere,
new green and white street signs,
Washington, New Jersey, and Maryland.
I remember that Ceci and I had to memorize
all the states and capitals last year.

Arrival

The turn signal clicks, trying to hypnotize me.
Stones smack against the tires.
I see the newer houses,
looking beige with white, brick so bare.

The tree

Daddy has promised me trees.
I cross my fingers on my one hand,
remember that two is bad luck,
like the time that I crossed twice when I
wanted to do a project with Ceci and
ended up with Wanda instead.

Mama pulls up to the curb and parks the car.
I look down.
The address painted on the curb: 1020 Pennsylvania.

"Look, baby, our new house. Look…"
Mama's hand is on my shoulder feeling
warm, but I don't want to feel it.

My shoulders are still hunched with unhappy.
The oak tree from our old backyard
is in the front yard.
Daddy dug it up last week.
It seems to be barely planted, some roots
sticking up and the leaves wilted.

It looks as uncomfortable as I feel.
I turn toward Mama, my eyes hard, like
marbles. "Transplants barely ever make it,"
I say under my breath.
Mama rolls the window down
and gathers up her purse

as Daddy comes to my door.
"You talk to her… I'm going in."

Daddy slides into the front seat.
I decide to stay in the car.
I don't plan on budging.
I sit in the car feeling like the tree.
It wants the dirt of my home, and I want it too.
I know the familiar house feeling I get when we park on
    our street
or when we pull into the alley.
I can't find my familiar.
I need a way to get back,
but right now I am stuck here, just like the tree.

My record collection of 45s

Daddy lets me sit, doesn't try to talk to me.
I look up finally and I see that
Jerome has my box marked *45s* and he's
about to drop them. I jump out of the car, run up to
    Jerome.
"Give them to me, Jerome… Come on."
Jerome barely listens. "Shoot, G, you don't have to be so
bossy."
"Mama, Jerome won't…"
The box starts to slip. I catch it.
Jerome taps me on the top of the head.
I grab at him.
A brochure for the Army falls
to the floor.
"What's that?"
"Nothing, Georgia, nothing…"

I enter the house, box in hand.
The smell of fresh paint makes me
cough, stings my eyes.
I get that tight feeling at the back
of my throat, like I suddenly need water.
I look around, emptiness,
no hardwood built-in nooks or cabinets.

I walk up to my new bedroom and set the box down.
My mattress is leaning against the wall.
The rest of the room is empty.
The five o'clock sun is shining through the windows.

I tip my bare mattress down to the floor,
lie on it and stare at the freshly painted
white ceiling, no cracks, no pictures,
just clean and blank.
I'm tired, I should help, but I don't.
My fingers touch the charm on the half of the heart
    necklace
that Ceci gave me from the Five & Dime.

I hold it and touch the jagged edge
that connects us together.
I close my eyes and remember
last week at Ceci's house,
dancing around her bedroom,
the record player blasting our song,
"R-E-S-P-E-C-T," our Aretha Franklin.

The kiss tree

At bedtime,
Mama comes up to kiss me on top of my head.
She gave me a kiss tree when I was two,
told me that every time she kissed me on top of
my head, my kiss tree would grow.
I know I'm too big for this kind of stuff now,
but I still lean my head forward for her to kiss.
I hug her quickly, since I'm so mad and I want her to
know.
I ask her to leave my door ajar, and I take my journal out.
I write by hallway light.
I look out the window and try to find
Ty's and my wishing star, but it seems that it's in the
wrong place and I can't see it.
I miss the sounds of home.
I write down what I can't hear.

The streetlight moon

The night sounds are very quiet here.
I can't hear Mr. Gregg on his porch listening to
Ernie Harwell calling the Tigers' plays.
Can't hear honking cars on Greenfield,
sirens, or motorcycles draggin' on 7 Mile.
Instead it's silent.
The streetlight shines into my room.
It's really only a pretend moon.

Sunday, June 18

Still there

I'm waking in the morning—in that space of
being awake enough to know I'm up but
not awake enough to not know where I am,
that feeling of empty that creeps up on you
and doesn't let go, that feeling that the minute you
stop thinking about everyone you love, they might
     disappear.

I look around and remember it's true—we've moved.
My box of records is by my closet.
I search for the change purse
from Aunt Birdie, find it, and inhale her perfume.

I walk downstairs and hear the radio playing
"Groovin' on a Sunday afternoon."
I smell coffee brewing.
I want to go outside, see where
I've landed.
"Mama, I'm going to sit on the porch."
"Breakfast, Georgia?"
"No, Mama, not hungry…"
I walk out the door.

The planting

Across the street there's a painted
garage door, a mural of deer in the woods, not like
Diego Rivera's Detroit Industry Murals
that we saw at the Detroit Institute of Arts for
our spring field trip this year.
This one looks more like paint by number
on velvet.

Squeak, Squeak, THUNK!
Looking in the direction of the sound,
I see a grandpa-age man with a yellow wheelbarrow.
I can't see any dirt piled in, no flowers,
no plants. I see a large bowling ball, purple swirled.
I wipe my eyes to make sure I'm seeing it.

He walks to the backyard to get a shovel and
then I see a kid. I can't tell if it's a boy or girl.
I hope a girl, a neighbor, a friend,
but Ceci doesn't dress like this.

This girl doesn't seem to care much for fashion—
she's wearing a Detroit Tigers hat, her thick, curly
black hair tied in a ponytail.
The old man leans over and whispers to her.
She begins to dig; she switches her hat brim
from front to back.

He's mixing cement. I can't help but stare.
The girl stirs, dust floats up, a powder of snow.
The girl and the man carefully lay it down.
They are planting a bowling ball.

Digging it up

I walk back into the house and wonder
why anyone would plant a bowling ball
in the front lawn and why anyone would
paint a mural on their garage. The painting's forest
is green, with blue tints of sky dancing through
the leaves.

This neighborhood looks so flat,
like a fresh sheet of paper.
Our house, the only
one here with older trees.
Our tree, my Detroit.
The tree left
a huge hole in my old backyard.
The houses here have silly
rounded shrubs, all green
and curvy.

The night the tree was dug up,
Mama went out to the backyard
in the middle of the night and tried
to fill that hole with dirt,
worried that if it rained
some kid might fall in and drown.
My dad said that my mama had
lost her head going out late at night.

Wondering why

It's early evening,
and I tug at Mama's shirt.
I need her to answer my question.
"Mama, why'd we move away from
Aunt Birdie and Ceci?" I start up again.
Jerome, my quiet brother, starts to pace.
He stands up and gets too close to my face.

"Georgia, what do you have to worry about?
You're only going into seventh grade. I was gonna
be on the varsity team and in my senior year.
No scout will be looking for me here.
Quit acting like a baby!"
Jerome brushes past me.
I slip and fall.
I can't tell if it's on purpose
or an accident, but the tears
start to come.

Not ready to be here

I run upstairs taking giant steps,
slam my door.
The door swings open, dents
my wall, leaving some plaster
on the floor. My face feels
hot with my mistake.

Mama's going to kill me,
but he started it…
"Georgia G, no slamming!"
I jump in my bed and hide under my covers.
I hear Gwendolyn Brooks's poem
about a secret place to go.
I turn the words in my head,
over and over again.
It sounds like a rhyme,
soothing.

Good-bye to Little Bit?

Will Ty even recognize me now?
I am tired of too many changes,
especially after all this tall that hit
me before all the other girls in my class.
I always want to win, but not this race to be a teen.

I can wait… My cousin Yvonne's always
talking about boys, clothes, hair, and makeup.
She's always hanging out at Northland Mall.
I am not interested in this.
I am hoping I don't grow another inch.
Each day I keep trying to balance books on
my head for posture, but deep down I wish
that gravity would pull the books down harder
and make me shorter.

Last year I could fit my legs lengthwise
in the bathtub, could have my feet
at a comfortable half of the couch,
with my feet only slightly overlapping
Jerome's feet.

I know where I am headed with
this height. Both of my parents are tall.
I don't want to use it for sports.
I know I will like it when I am all grown but
now I feel like the Statue of Liberty.
The kids at my old school were always trying to
jump to my height and ask me stupid
questions like, "How's the climate up there,
Jolly Green Giant? Ho, ho, ho…"

Hair fight

I am still mad at Mama about the hair fight
we had last week. Mama agreed to let me have
two ponytail braids, but she said no hair straightening
until junior high. I have to wear it natural.
I will stand out enough being tall
and Black in this neighborhood.
If Ty were here, he couldn't call me his "Little Bit"
    anymore.

I can stay home alone

We haven't turned on the air yet.
Daddy likes the windows open anyways.
Mama knocks at the door, tells me she'll
help me unpack, her way of a quiet apology.
We were calm, but we start back up again.

We begin to unpack and argue.
She wants me being looked after in the morning
when she goes to work.
I think I can stay home by myself.
"It's summer! I want to hang out, listen to records,
roller-skate, Hula-Hoop, ride my bike.
Mama, I don't need to be watched."
I try to convince her but there's no arguing
with her.

We reach a compromise, and I agree
to go to the Camp Kennedy School near our house
for the morning if I can hang out in the afternoon
at home. I'm acting like it's a choice.
I know she's already signed me up.

The phone

It's now Sunday night before
Mama goes back to work and
my official start of summer.

I walk quietly toward the
hallway phone. I practice
picking up the receiver and
setting it down gently
to see if anyone can hear me
click the receiver down.

I feel guilty.
I should tell Aunt Birdie about the contest,
let her know that I borrowed her address.
I am not sure that I want to tell her but know I should.

I am practicing for later tonight
when I call.
I need to hear her voice.
I can still hear her telling
me to be brave.

I know she'll start
whooping and hollering
when she hears me.
I wait in the hall.
Jerome jumps down the last three steps and
smacks me on the head.
I will not complain now, don't want to

get caught talking on the phone.
When he comes closer, I just glare at him,
giving him my just-you-wait look…

How Kow Chinese

Mama's still in the kitchen, trying to find dishes
from boxes when Daddy comes in with
Chinese food from the restaurant
that's in the neighborhood.
Chicken fried rice, my favorite.
He has remembered the sweet and sour sauce and
    chopsticks.
I almost forget to be mad.

We don't usually eat in front of the TV, but tonight's
    different.
Daddy opens his fortune cookie and reads,
"When hungry, eat more Chinese food."
We all laugh for the first time in a while.
I open my fortune cookie and read,
"Now is the time to try something new."
I fold it up, put it in my pocket, and
wonder if Mama has unpacked her
typewriter yet...

After dinner I sit down next to my daddy,
and we watch the Walt Disney Sunday
night movie *Atta Girl Kelly*.
I saw it a few months ago, about a boy
training a seeing-eye dog.
I like this kind of movie but I can't
sit still.
I want to call Aunt Birdie.

I sneak down the hall, carefully pick
up the phone, hold my hand over the
receiver to muffle the sound.
My fingers dial. I wait for
the tone to go to the next number.
All seven complete. I barely
breathe and then hear the busy signal.
I feel choked up, don't try again,
run upstairs, grab my writing notebook,
slide the back screen door
open, and begin to learn my backyard
and write...

The light show

The fireflies have come out.
There are only a few at first. They seem to
be sending signals.
One lonely one and then two.
The backyard seems to light up some more.
The fireflies blink, on and off and on and off,
like a heat lightning storm.
I hear a cricket symphony.
I remember the time
last summer when Ceci caught
ten that lit up the glass jar.

Surrender

I can't find a container to put the fireflies in
with all the boxes scattered inside.
I carefully cup my hands
and watch the light show on my palms.

After a bit, Mama comes
out and tells me I need to go in,
wash off my feet, get ready for
tomorrow. I start to complain, take it
back, knowing I won half the argument to stay
home in the afternoon.
I surrender instead.

Daddy knocks

Daddy knocks on the door.
He's not one for chatting.
He smiles soft. I look down and see
he's holding a big roll of wide tape
and a wrapping paper tube.
He hands the tube to me.
Inside are two maps—a world one and a local one.
I put my arms around his neck, hug briefly.

"Which wall, baby?" I point to behind my bed.
"I'll hold this side." The map starts to curl back up.
"Here, let's do the trick and roll it backwards."
He's gentle and strong at the same time.
For years I watched him draw
on tissue paper-like plans with a special pen,
not tearing through the paper,
making blue lines.

We make tape loops, place the maps above my bed.
We don't flatten it in case it's crooked.
We both like things to be exact.

"There, all done." Daddy smacks his hands together,
hands me pin tacks and string.
I look at the scale, measure with my fingertips how far
we are from Ty in Vietnam—8,458 miles.
I wind 'round the string on the tack, knot it.
I place another tack on Detroit and one on Saigon,
Vietnam.

When Daddy leaves, I attach a shorter string from
Southfield to Detroit,
Aunt Birdie and Ceci's house only miles away,
but it feels like a long distance to me...

The day camp

Mama walks me over to
the summer school program
before she leaves for work.

I kick a rock slowly,
watch it tumble toward
the fence, getting stuck
under the rail.

I slow my walk, hoping she will
change her mind.

She didn't really listen last night.
I tried to convince her. "I'm old enough to stay home
this summer. I'm a sixth-grade graduate.
I'm not a baby."
"You're not a baby, you're *my* baby."

There's no arguing with her
when she's made her mind up and tells me to
save my defense for law school.

Many are gone

The school sign reads "Kennedy Elementary School."
There's a gigantic gold emblem of President John F.
    Kennedy above the door,
a memorial for when he was killed,
just four years ago, when I was eight.
I remember coming home and seeing Mama's eyes.
Mama doesn't cry often, only at weddings
and at my uncle Russell's funeral.

We met Uncle Russell's casket at Detroit Metro Airport
this past November.
That's the same airport that Ty flew out of last summer.
Mama said I could stay in school that day.
I didn't want to be sad at school, or cry,
even if Ceci's desk was next to mine.
I didn't want that counselor lady to pull
me from class and ask about my feelings.
She doesn't know me.

The coffin was draped with the American flag,
which they carefully folded into a triangle
and handed to Mama, since she's the big sister.
At first Mama put it in the living room, but
it got her too sad so she put it somewhere safe.

Camp Kennedy

The door's open and I can see lanyards,
craft supplies, and a woman with a long braid
and a shirt that says "Flower Power."
My eyes walk in but I want to walk out.

The Flower Power woman greets us,
tells us her name's Misty and hands Mama a form.
There are a few kids playing with
a wooden hockey box on the table,
one younger kid and one older kid
with curly hair and a Tigers hat.
She's jumping up and down for
every goal, shouting, "Yes! Score!"

I can hardly hear Mama telling them
I'm allowed to leave on my own in the
afternoon when my brother's home.
Mama tries to reach for
me and tell me it's okay. "Mama, please," I beg.
My voice sounds low and wolf-like.
"Please, Mama, I don't want to be here."
She kisses me.
"Georgia, stop now… See you tonight."

Misty is really nice and tries to
ask about what I like to do.
She's trying hard, but I've got
no try in me.

I should be with Aunt Birdie,
helping with the pickles and sorting
out the cosmetics for the Mary Kay bags.

A few more kids straggle in,
get paper, start making cootie catchers.
I don't want to stare but turn around
and see the girl with the baseball cap.
She looks up at me.

"How long are you in here for?"
She sounds as pleased as I feel.
It feels like a summer jail sentence.
"The morning, I guess. I can leave after lunch."
I think this is the girl from down the street,
from the bowling ball house.

She shoots out her hand like a grown-up to
shake hands.
"Naomi," she says and points to her Detroit Tigers hat.
"Georgia," I say and give her a half-bent smile.

All day

We are the oldest kids here.
I spend the rest of the morning
drawing pictures for the little kids,
while Naomi kicks a kickball back and forth
with another kid.

This summer I was going to get paid to watch
Stacy and Tracy, the twins down the block
at my old house.
Instead I'm playing with these kids for free,
and I feel like I'm being babysat
by the Flower Power counselor.
She's nice and knows I'm older and treats
me different than the others.

When I get home

At the end of the day
Mama's home early.
"How's your day, baby?"
"Okay, I guess."
"Boy, I was almost late today
driving that distance." Mama sounds tired.
"Maybe we shouldn't have moved.
It would have been easier," I mumble as I go
upstairs because being alone
feels better than making small talk.
If anyone wants to see me, they'll
have to find me first.

Tuesday, June 20

Getting to know you

Today I walk to camp on my own.
Naomi runs up to me.
"I'm saving up S&H green stamps
from the Mobil gas station to buy a new baseball mitt."
Naomi talks fast, pacing back and forth.
She barely takes a breath or stops moving,
just like the boxer
Muhammad Ali, the Champ, six times Golden
Gloves champion. My brother Ty and
I used to watch him all the time.

She glances back at me.
"It's just Mom, Grandpa Herman, and me since Dad
moved out. Do you have brothers or sisters?"

"I have two. My brother Jerome, he's in twelfth grade.
My brother Ty's in Vietnam."
I say it slowly and quietly, don't want that
peace sign counselor to hear this.

"My brother Jerome's really good at baseball.
He was playing varsity and does some pitching.
The coach didn't agree with my parents' decision to move
    going into his senior year.
He's working for Parks and Rec and will be coaching
    the boys' team."

I feel strange—this is more than I've said to
anyone this week.
"Boys' team and me, then…that's my team."

Naomi squints and puts her hand up
to block the sun.
"Why'd ya move if he was going to play varsity?"
"I don't know, and my parents are keeping
it a secret."
I start thinking about Ty, Jerome, and Detroit.
I'm about to answer, but she has already
taken off for the baseball diamond.
The fields are surrounded by concrete walls
with apartments on the other side.

I think about boxing and Ty and say to myself,
"Float like a butterfly and sting like a bee,"
 as Muhammad Ali would say.

I go back inside, help one of the younger girls
do the box stitch with the lanyard.
After lunch I stay, work in the craft corner.
I don't want to face my new house today.

The poster

I don't need to use the key
to get in. Mama's home,
but I race upstairs. Jerome's
door's open and I see the boxing
poster of Muhammad Ali already
up in his new room.

I've been thinking about
how my daddy said that Ali should stop
boxing if he can't fight for his country.

I reach into my sock drawer,
find my journal, where I keep
my secrets.

I find my contest poem.
The Spirit of Detroit,
It can shake, it can shimmy, it's the Motown sound...
It makes me happy and sad at the same time and then
I feel a bit sick to my stomach.
I need a plan to get back to Aunt Birdie's,
to look in her mailbox before she does,
to see if I won. I need to tell her what I did.
Would she understand?

Ask Jerome

I'll ask Jerome if I can go with him when
he plays ball on Saturday in Detroit.
I'll pay attention to the bus route and take
notes in case I decide to go back
on my own, without him,
since this is really too soon
for the contest envelope to arrive.
It's only been a week.

How not to win a poetry contest

Know the rules.
Act as if you don't know or
understand them.

Use your aunt's address, even
though you don't live with her.

Keep it a secret from your mama,
even though up to this point
you have never kept anything
from her
ever.

Wednesday, June 21

Beg to stay home

Mama comes to wake me. I fake sleep.
She's getting mad and is ready to leave for work.
"Come on, Georgia. I've got an early class to teach
and Jerome's coaching."

"Not today, Mama, please…"
"Just today. Back to camp tomorrow."
"Mama, you know that I was going to
babysit this summer, not *be* babysat!"
I hear her sigh heavy as she leaves the room,
and she doesn't close the door quietly.

What I really want to do today is sleep in and
talk to Ceci on the phone.

When I'm sure Mama's gone, I go
downstairs, eat cereal out of the box,
search for the prize.

Yesterday's paper

I see the *Detroit Free Press* still folded
on the table.
It's yesterday's. It looks like it hasn't even moved
from the counter.
I read the headline:
"Muhammad Ali Convicted of Refusing
Induction in Armed Services."
I'm not sure what *induction* means but
I know he's not going to go.

Air mail

I search around for the thin
aerogram tissue-like mailers
to write to Ty.

Dear Ty,

Your hero, Muhammad Ali,
is refusing to be drafted
to go to Vietnam.

Daddy's getting so mad.
He keeps saying,
"How can a prize fighter
not be willing to fight?"
I am trying to understand
about peace and war and
to understand what's right
and what's wrong.

We see some of the war
on TV but Daddy doesn't
let me watch.

I keep looking for your
face, even though I know
it is impossible to find you.

How can a fighter not
believe in fighting?

Love you,

Just me...Little Bit

I grab my journal and continue to write.
I remember looking through
Daddy's *Detroit Free Press* with Ty,
scissors in hand.

Ransom poems with Ty

Writing ransom poems with Ty,
taking Daddy's newspapers and scissors and
searching for words and cutting them out.
Words I could read, like **is** and **was** and **were**.
Searching for sounds that I heard, like **bird** and
sing and **song**.
Searching for what I saw, like **tree** and **branch** and
bud.

Should I **write** a **ransom poem** to Aunt Birdie,
give her **clues**, send her a **secret** message
about my **lie?**

I chicken in instead

Even though I wanted to go out
and explore, I chicken out
instead and stay in and watch TV.

No one is home for the day, so
I am going to be the queen of the TV,
no one to argue with.

First is *The Dating Game*.
I always write down who I think the
match will be.

The questions are ridiculous and
stupid. I'm glad to take my mind off
missing Aunt Birdie, Ceci, and Ty.

I like *Candid Camera*. It's just stupid fun,
catching people in the act of doing pranks and
stuff.

The last show before lunch is *The Andy Griffith Show*,
about a small-town sheriff who lives with his
aunt Bea and his son, Opie, but it's a
small town, much smaller than Southfield.
Aunt Bea brings me to Aunt Birdie, and by the
end of the show, I'm sad and remember
where I am.
This TV escape has backfired on me.
Maybe camp is not so bad after all.

If Jerome won't let me tag along

Our new basement is not as
creepy as our old basement—
less spider webs, no hanging bare
light bulbs, no strange creaky noises
going down the steps.

If Jerome won't let me tag along,
I can begin to figure out some of this
on my own.
Daddy has lots of maps and plans
in the basement, rolled up
like Christmas wrapping paper.
I like the feel of the onion skin,
see-through tracing paper.
The blue mimeograph in perfect
lines and measurements.
I like this certainty.

The AAA maps are kept in
a special box.
I fold and unfold them, one
at a time.
I find the Detroit city map.
He won't miss this one.
I find 8 Mile and follow it
across with my finger.

I bring it upstairs and
hide it under my bed.

Back to day camp

I'm not sure why, but I'm
happy to see the little kids.
I've only been gone a day, and two kids
come up and give me a big hug,
almost knocking me down,
asking me where I was yesterday.

Naomi says, "Hey," asks me
if I want to watch team practice
by the backstop, way down at the
cinderblock wall that
divides the school from the apartments.

A few of the kids beg to watch.
Misty says I can take all that I can hold in
my hands, so two of the little ones walk with me, glued
to my side.

Jerome and Naomi being buds

It's practice, so it's a bit slower for
the little kids. I let them run around
in the grass.

Jerome and Naomi are acting as if
they have known each other for a while.
They've only had three practices, and the first
game's tomorrow. I can't tell if he's working
more with her because she's a girl on an all-
boys team or the fact that she's pretty darn good.

She's alternating fielding between first and
short-stop. She can throw like no girl I've seen.
She makes it look easy as the ball
flies through the air like Artemis's arrows.
Maybe she's the sister Jerome was
supposed to have…
I miss Ty…

Not my first white kid

Naomi's not the first white kid
I've played with. There was Daddy's work
friend Don and his wife, Suzy,
who had two kids Jerome's and my age,
Shirley and Scott.
They'd come over a couple of times a year.
Usually in November to watch the Thanksgiving
parade, the Santa event at city hall,
and the annual summer picnic at Belle Isle.

They told my daddy about our house,
even though they live on the other side
of Mt. Vernon, the gravel street that
divides the subdivisions, five blocks down.

It used to be that sometimes
they would come by
on weekends or we'd go to their house.
But they were polite friends,
not the kind of friends that
you have to find on your own,
not knowing which games they'd want
to play.

When Ceci and I play, we can
always finish each other's sentences,
and we can usually go most of the
morning just reading each other's
thoughts.

Mama's home...not mine

I am feeling kind of mad and want to pick
a fight, so I push into the living room.
"Mama, why'd we have to move?" I tug at her shirt,
feel like I'm five. "Mama, why? I'm miserable here…
Why now before the contest winners were announced?"
My voice is beginning to have that dry, cracking
feeling before you cry.
"Georgia. What contest?"
"The Spirit of Detroit Poetry Contest."
She doesn't ask and I don't tell her.
Mama turns to me and gathers me up.
"I know it's hard, baby…"
Today this hug will just have
to be enough.
"Go wash up for dinner now…
and remember tomorrow you go
back to camp."

Friday, June 23

In which we escape to home

Naomi looks at Misty and says,
"Bye." This is the first time I feel
free and scared at the same time.
When we get past the gate, we both say,
"See you tomorrow." We both look back
and half wave.

I'm ready for a choice at lunch.
Hanging with the little guys has taken away
my urge to eat sandwiches.
Mama has bought a bunch of Swanson TV dinners.

Jerome's outside shooting baskets and says, "Hey."
Mama doesn't mind me using the oven
when Jerome's home. I gotta tell him
when I turn it on and that I turn it off.
Her sister, Birdie, used the oven too young
and got a scar, so Mama's extra careful.

I open the fridge, and the cool mist
wraps around me. I pick up the first TV dinner—
Salisbury steak, peas, fruit compote, and mashed
potatoes; then chicken, potatoes, mixed vegetables,
and apple cobbler;
then macaroni, spiced pears,
green beans, and pudding.

The thought of warm pudding on a hot day is not a good
one. This food looks like what the astronauts
ate on Gemini 12.
It's wrapped in a tight foil,
and doesn't even look like food.
I peel back the foil and wait for the magic.

I choose chicken, since I'm not wanting
to figure out the whole Salisbury steak thing.
I set the timer for twenty-five minutes,
run upstairs to get a copy of my contest poem.

A long time ago I watched Mrs. Serelli, two doors
down, plant a picture of St. Joseph in her backyard.
"He's the saint for houses," she said.
I slide the screen door and go out,
and I decide to plant my poem.

Planting my poem under our tree

I read the second line.
R-E-S-P-E-C-T, Aretha,
it's time to go downtown.

I take the paper,
fold it in half,
in quarters,
and finally in eighths,
until it is the size of
a peach pit.

I dig around close to the
tree's roots,
plant my words,
cover them with dirt.
Remember Miss Brooks's
poem about Skipper, the goldfish
buried under the old garden tree.

I look up at the sky,
careful not to ask
God to win,
try to not have a selfish
thought, like Aunt Birdie
taught me, when saying
a prayer or making a request.

I say four words,
"Please let me win."

I imagine my poem
being painted on a wall
in my city, Detroit, not here.

I look up, and the
clouds become my mural.
The wind erases them, and with
one big gust
they leave.

Hula-Hoop

I wipe my hands on my shorts and look
in the garage for my Hula-Hoop.
I got pretty good this last summer with Ceci.
She has one that has beads in it.
You can hear the beads go 'round, even
when it stops.

I gather up the hoop. It makes me feel sad,
remembering our timed contests. One time
around my waist, 100. Then Ceci was a show-
off and got 102 times.
We fell out laughing and then
couldn't even do a rematch to twenty.
It's real hard to Hula-Hoop and laugh.

Calling Ceci

I go back inside to call Ceci. I get her mom.
She asks about me and Mama, Daddy, and Jerome.
I'm not sure if she forgets about Ty
or just doesn't want to ask.
I act all casual, like things are great.
She says Ceci's out with Wanda. My heart skips
a beat, and it's hard to catch my breath.
These words are like a punch in the gut.

Wanda…Wanda. Ceci doesn't even like her.
It makes me feel good and bad at the same time.
Good that I can't be replaced
but bad that she's trying to see if I can.
I tell her mama that the oven timer has gone off.
I don't want her asking too many
more questions. I say, "Thank you, Mrs. Stephens,"
and hang up before I sound like I'm hiding a cry.

The oven goes off and I grab the oven mitts,
shout out to Jerome that the oven's off,
set the tray down carefully on the counter,
sit on the new barstools that face into the kitchen.

While lunch is cooling I go upstairs to get my
poetry journal to keep me company.
I think about Gwendolyn Brooks and how
I want to show her around my Detroit.

To Miss Brooks

I want to be your tour guide
take you to my school.
I want you to meet
Mrs. Murphy, who read
us your Bronzeville Boys and Girls,
who told us about your Chicago neighborhood,
like my Detroit.
A song, a jump rope rhyme,
with a beat in the city, your Chicago and mine.

I finish lunch and tuck my poetry journal under my
pillow.

The circus dog

I hear a bark and see Naomi with her dog.
I'm not so lonely that I feel a need to
go over there and hang out.
We spent the morning together.
As Mama says, I'm old enough
to entertain myself.

I pick up the Hula-Hoop again
and try it around my wrist.
The hoop begins to go 'round again and again,
like the moon orbits
the earth.
I transfer the hoop to my left hand, then ankle.
It drops on the ground,
and I jump in and out like the bell hop toy
I got for my birthday last year.

I stop, wipe the sweat off, hear
applause that brings me back to here and now.
I look up. Naomi's clapping.
"Know any other circus tricks?"
I'm embarrassed and don't care
all at the same time.

"Jax knows a few. Toss me the hoop."
I flip the hoop over and it gets stuck
on top of the fence.

Naomi grabs the hoop, holds it sideways.

I almost expect her to light it on fire.
Jax looks up at her impatiently with a
slight tail wag. He's a mutt but seems
like a nice dog. His fur's mostly white with
stamps of orange and black.

She gives Jax a hand signal.
He jumps through the hoop.
Each time she raises it a bit higher and praises him
and gives him a treat. Now I'm the one
who's clapping.

"How'd he learn to do that?"
"I'm grooming him for *The Ed Sullivan Show*.
I want to get us both on TV. If not national,
maybe *Bozo's Big Top* in Windsor."
"What else can he do?"
Naomi holds up a biscuit and he stands on
his hind legs and turns in a circle, sits, and barks.
The sitting trick isn't amazing,
but the standing part is pretty cool.

She's still standing outside my fence.
I tell her to go around by the other side of the
gate, and I let her and Jax into our backyard.

I prepare myself to be met by this dog.
He seems smart, but I'm not much of
a dog person on account of getting bit
by a neighbor's dog when I was five.
She looks up, tilts her hat back, and extends
it down.

"This here is Jax, the wonder dog!"
He sits, gives a paw to shake.
Jax seems better than the dogs I've known,
and he's smart and obedient and can
do circus tricks.
He bounds over to me,
knocking me over a bit, and he goes for
my mouth and tries to lick me...
No way... I get up in time.

How to make a friend

Be interested in this new girl,
even though she's not your type.
Know that she will never be like
Ceci.

Pretend to like dogs.
Keep your face away so he never
licks you.

Jerome, please...

"Jerome, please can I go
back with you to Detroit on Saturday?
You told Mama that you were meeting
the guys for a game."
I am jumping up and down now
like a small yappy dog, and he's treating
me like one.
He puts his hand on my head
and motions. "Shhh…"
"Why not? You already told Mama
that you were going."
"Georgia, I just made up the part
about playing ball with the guys.
I have to meet with someone else."
"Tell me. I promise I won't tell."

"It's nothing, G., but Mama said you
had to wait at least a week to see friends
so you can adjust. Who're you going to hang with?"
"No plans. I just need to see something."

He finally agrees.
I wonder why he needs to lie to me?
We've never kept secrets.

Ceci, meet me at the Five & Dime

I sneak to the phone,
carefully lift the phone receiver,
and listen to the dial tone.
Ceci recognizes my voice right away,
gets all excited, starts to shout for
her mama to share the news.
"Mama, it's—"
If I was with her, I'd slap my hand over
her mouth like the time that she
almost told Westin that I liked him.
"Ceci, no, don't tell her.
Mama doesn't know; she'd be so mad if
she found out. Please don't say anything to anyone."
We plan to meet at the Five & Dime, and I will
see her after I check Aunt Birdie's mailbox.

Saturday, June 24

Do I tell Ceci today?

We leave early while Mama sleeps in.
Daddy's at work.
Jerome and I walk to the bus stop.
He's got enough change. I look to see
how much money I might need.
I know Aunt Birdie gave me change
too, but I act like I forgot it.
"Jerome, how much?"
"I got it, G. That's what
big brothers are for."
I try to watch as I hear
the clank of the coins
hit the metal and slide down
the glass chute.

I take out my notebook,
crane my neck, read
street names.
"Georgia, why are you
so up and down?
Sit still. People are starting
to look at you."
Jerome seems a bit nervous too.
I'm not sure why. He has a folder
under his arm, and he seems to have
forgotten his mitt.

"Jerome, where's your baseball stuff?"

He drops me at the Five & Dime and tells
me he'll pick me up at two.
Now I have a long way to walk to
Aunt Birdie's house and then back to
meet Ceci here at twelve.

I have to be sneaky, but I already know
that Aunt Birdie is always out on
Saturdays. She does her "weeklies."

First she stops at Eastern Market, early,
comes back home, puts produce away,
then out again to the Detroit Institute of Arts, or meeting
with the girls, as she says.

I go around back to see if her back door
is open, duck behind the bushes
in case there's movement.
Coast clear. I go to the front.
Know it's probably too early.
I open the metal box.
The lid creaks that sharp,
high-pitched squeak.

A bill from J.L. Hudson's
department store and some
newspapers and advertisements.
I look around me, feel like a spy,
hide back by her front shrubs.
I don't want the neighbors to know
I'm here.

I know it's too early for the contest
announcement.
Time seems long since we moved.
I know it's still June, and I know
I don't live here anymore.

My old house that's not mine

Before I leave, I go around to the alley
where our old house and Aunt
Birdie's met back to back,
the alley between the houses.

I see two kids in my old backyard,
playing on my old lawn.

They are not us
anymore.

Five & Dime, Ceci, and feeling fine

I see her down the block.
We both rush up, give a
hug like it's been years
and scream as if we're at recess.

She's back from her week at
her grandma's. She'll be
back and forth most of the summer.

She starts talking fast.
I can barely get a word in.
I really want to hear more
from her anyways.
Her folks are good, and
her brothers are as irritating
as ever.
She's watching them when her
Daddy sleeps during the day, since
he has nightshift. My daddy
said the Detroit police officers
are all staying home because they
don't want to write eighty tickets a
day. My daddy showed me the newspaper
with the headline *Blue Flu*.

We go in, split a Sanders
hot fudge cream puff,
and I'm back home.

Time to go and cross our hearts

Jerome shows up,
pats us on our
heads and says, "Hey!" to Ceci.
"We gotta go now."
In my happiness, I have
forgotten my other home
is not here.

We hug
again
and
again
and again
until Jerome
pulls me away.

No envelope

He's missing the large manila
envelope that he brought today.
I wonder why but don't ask.
I don't have the contest envelope
either—the one I'd hoped to find.
"Jerome, where's that envelope from this morning?"
"Don't worry, Georgia, I took care of it."

Sunday, June 25

"Muhammad Ali sentenced to five years for evading the draft."

The *Detroit News* headline shouts at me
early Sunday morning.
Daddy and I used to get up early, and he'd make me
"coffee"—mostly cream—and we would
pick one article to discuss and then
make Mama breakfast because, as
Daddy says, she cooks all week.
But this morning I glance at Daddy and he's staring
through me.

Monday, June 26

Peace mosaic

Misty has promised us that
today is the day that we will make
a mosaic with her. Since we are older,
she's trying to have some cool
stuff for us. We have to wear safety
goggles as we chip away at the tiles.
She wants to make a mosaic that
says *Peace Not War*.
I don't tell her that my brother is in Vietnam,
because I also believe in peace
and not war. We use heavy gloves
to pick up all the pieces,
careful not to get cut with the jagged glass.
I touch Ceci's necklace, wonder about her and Wanda,
take a deep breath, sign out, and walk home.

After camp and rice paper mail

I race to the mailbox. I'm hoping for a letter
from Ty or Aunt Birdie.

I feel the metal, warm on top from the sun
and yet cool inside in the darkness.
It feels empty. Then my hand
reaches a thin envelope, and I know it has flown far...
The letter looks like rice paper candy that I have
tasted when Mama goes to Pier 1.
I see the Aero Mail from overseas—Vietnam.

I know I'm not allowed
to open it. The paper and envelope,
all in one, tear too easily,
like a fall leaf disintegrating.

X-ray vision

I hold the letter to the light,
can see Ty's signature.
His *Y* always wraps around
to the top of his *T*, making
his name look all curvy and fancy.

I am hoping that
Mama will let me keep
the lotus blossom stamp.
I've started to collect
these stamps but know I
shouldn't ask for it right away.

When letters come,
her hand shakes, and Daddy
sits with her, takes the envelope,
reads
each word of
each sentence
with a strong breath
that could blow out a candle.

My daddy reads

Mama waits until dinner is over,
holds the letter while my daddy reads.
Ty is in the city on leave,
says he will send pictures soon.
He describes the city, the lights,
the colors, the smells.
There are a few Vietnamese characters at the end of
the page. They might as well be a code
because none of us know what they say.
I trace my fingers over the characters,
slowly,
and run to my room,
take out my journal, and write.

The rhythm of it

Sometimes the truth looks different
in the daylight.
Brighter, clear, or loud.
Sometimes a secret can be quiet,
or steady, like the metronome
beat, like when Ty took
piano lessons and I would
watch and tap my feet.

Our star

When the stars come out,
I push the blinds aside,
let the blinking lights of planes
pass as I see the stars against
blue-black skies.
I find Ty's and my wishing star
and send him a wish.

After camp: Efros Drug Store

"Wanna ride bikes to Efros Drug Store
and get some Bazooka bubble gum?" Naomi
asks, squinting shut one eye as she looks
into the blinding sun.

"We didn't bring my old bike—it's
too small—so I can't ride with you…"
I'm hoping for one on my birthday, July Fourth.
When I was little, my daddy used to tell me the
fireworks were just for me.

"Jerome, I'm going over to Naomi's
to get her bike and then going riding."

"Okay, Little Bit, but don't let Mama catch you
riding on the seat. She'll be steamed."
I get mad. Only Ty gets to call me Little Bit.
Naomi takes Jax to the backyard.
We go around to the front,
walk through her door.
I look up at the doorpost,
see a little ceramic piece with unusual symbols on it.
"What's this?
"It's a mezuzah. It keeps the house safe.
It's in all Jewish houses.
We have one on the front and back door,

by our bedrooms.
It has a prayer scroll in it."

"Do all Jewish people have them in their houses?"
"Most of the houses in this neighborhood.
There's a lot of kids on this block
that go to my Hebrew school.
I'm trying to get out of it, but my mom wants
me to have a bat mitzvah.
I thought my ticket out was
when I squirted my teacher,
Mrs. Greenbaum, with a squirt gun last year,
but I didn't get a Get Out of Jail Free card."
The entrance looks just like my house.
The rooms are all in the same place.
Her grandpa's half-asleep watching TV.

"Grandpa, I'm going on a bike ride with Georgia."
"Okay, bubbelah," he says and goes back to sleep.
Naomi pushes the electric garage door opener.

"I've got a blue Schwinn banana seat. We can
both ride on mine."
Naomi returns with her bike in tow.
"Hop on."
I grab the sissy bar on the back tightly.
She stands up to get some speed.
I've been used to hopping on and off since I was little.
Jerome used to have me sit on the top of his handlebars
if Mama and Daddy weren't
looking, so I'm a good balancer.

New Orleans Mall

It's hot and muggy today, my shirt clinging to my
back like it's magnetic. We stop outside some shops
with a courtyard in the middle. There's a shoe store,
a bakery, a restaurant named Dubbs, the shopping center
grocery store at the end.
The bakery has neon lights that say *kosher*,
like at Mr. Weiss's Deli by Aunt Birdie's house.
But the stores are all in a rectangle, a small mall, not
like the shops all lined up on
the streets of Detroit.

We walk into the store that says Efros.
It's a small store with the pharmacy in the back,
smells like a cross between soap and medicine.
Naomi takes me over to the candy aisle.
I have pocket change from
cleaning my room and helping with the unpacking.

I am thinking about getting the candy necklace,
chocolate cigarettes, Sugar Babies, Sweet Tarts,
or Chuckles.

Eyes on us

I notice that the store lady is standing down
the aisle, looking over her glasses at us.
She focuses her eyes on me
and tells me that I can use this green plastic
basket to put my purchases in. Naomi tries to use
her baseball cap. The woman's mouth gets all tight and
prune-like. She walks on by. Two boys are hanging out
in the aisle and staring at us.

Naomi elbows me. "That's just Joey. He was in my class
last year, and he's on my team.
He's just acting stupid, like most of the boys."
Naomi points down the aisle.
"That's his mom, talking to Mrs. Cohen."
I can hear Mrs. Cohen whisper too loud, and she points
to me now.
"They're living in the Goldstein place," Mrs. Cohen says.
"Mira never even said they were leaving. You know the
zoning law—no For Sale signs… It's as if
they left in the middle of the night." I try not
to hear, but it's too late.

I feel like I don't belong here. The excitement
of the candy is dwindling. Naomi pats me hard
on the back and motions toward the counter
to pay. I hand my change to the cashier and take
the bag outside.

Bubblegum challenge

Naomi gets out her Bazooka bubble gum, gives
me a piece, and we sit down on the
bench and have a bubble-blowing contest.
"The rules are simple—the largest bubble wins.
The trick is that the bubble has to be able to be
taken out of your mouth so we can tell which is bigger."

My first one is loud and pops like a
mini Fourth of July. Naomi blows one pretty good,
but I want to outmatch her. We keep going back
and forth, and I don't know what gets into me…

She blows another one, and then I lift my hand and pop
    it into her face.
Naomi shouts out, "Hey!" and wipes it off
and begins to chase me around the inside of the courtyard.
I dodge between the planters.
We finally stop, hot and exhausted,
let the sweat drip down.
Now we need a Coke.

We ride across the street and stop at the Mobil gas station,
find the rest of our change. We don't have much left, so
we split the Coke. Naomi sets the bike down by
the air machine, and we sit on the cement curb.

The bottle's sweating and dripping down.
I reach up to my forehead with my cool hand.
We gotta get back soon.

I try to balance the Coke in one hand
and hold on with the other. Naomi stops the
bike here and there to take a swig.

I ask her to stop down the street,
so I can get off.
Mama doesn't like me riding
double—she's told me many times.
Naomi sits on her bike, her feet padding
pavement.
I walk alongside.
We wave as we each go home for dinner.

Evening baseball in the street

After dinner the sun's going
down slowly. The Orange Crush-like
pink sky is lost to the apartments behind
the school wall. It's getting too dark to head
to the playground, but I see Naomi out
with a couple of neighborhood kids.
Jerome is right behind me and pushes through,
saying, "Go on, slowpoke. I'm gonna play
ball." I am not eager and sit on the porch.
The teams are uneven so they call me over.

They gather in the street to play as they toss bases down,
a hat for home. Jerome knows most of these
kids from coaching his Little League team.

Right field and prayers

I don't want to play. In Detroit, Jerome never wants
me to. He must be desperate, but they need even
teams. I play right field, which means I'm
down the street a bit.
I figure I can pray that Jerome and Naomi will be off,
won't hit that far.
I'm on Naomi's team with a kid with
bright red curly hair and his brother, who has a buzz
cut and a beanie on his head with a star.
On Jerome's team he's got a kid with black frizzy
hair. I think that's Joey, the kid from the drugstore.
I'm glad he's not on my team.

They show me the hand signal if a car comes by.
As evening comes, the street lights
flicker slowly, dull at first, like the
dimmer switch in our old dining room,
now bright like a movie spotlight,
and with it, mosquitoes
and the last humidity of the day.

A cool treat

Naomi's grandpa's sitting outside
on his lawn chair with his transistor, listening
to the Tigers home game.
I can hear the static,
the muffled cheers of the crowd.

The Good Humor truck comes by and we have
Jerome tell them to wait as we all run home to
get permission and money from our rooms.

I already have plans for a chocolate éclair
ice cream bar, and I know Jerome will have the
toasted almond bar.

The lights start to sound like cicadas buzzing.
We know that means it's getting too dark
to be out, and we know better. Come home before dark.

Thursday, June 29

A Ceci surprise at night

The phone rings. I race down the hall.
It's Ceci's mama wanting to talk to my mama.
I tell her that she will call back.
I wait expectantly, wondering why they need to talk.

I try to sneak behind Mama when she calls back.
Sounds like I might have my first sleepover in
my new house, or maybe even go back to Detroit.
"Sure, Georgia can come to visit Ceci."
Music to my ears.
"Mama, when, Mama?"
I jump up and down screaming.
"Georgia! You're acting like a five-year-old not
able to wait. I'll take you to Aunt Birdie's
after work, baby."
Mama's now seeing the happy girl she forgot about.

Friday, June 30

Peace is hidden

The next day at camp we finish
up our mosaics. The words *Peace Not War*
glitter from the tiles. I bring mine
home after lunch and hide it
in my closet toward the back and
cover it with a towel.
Mama and Daddy can't think I'm a
war protester.

After I hide it well,
I get out my journal.

"My family is a mosaic"

We are so many different pieces,
in parts.
Aunt Birdie and Ceci in Detroit.
A piece of us so far away in Vietnam.

A jagged edge to the side.
I do not know the jungles
of Vietnam, the rice paddies,
the war.
My family is a mosaic
in pieces.

Back to Detroit and a visit with Ceci

Mama tells me to get ready to go.
I hide my journal under my pillow
and pack. So much hiding, so many secrets.

I get clean clothes for tomorrow, check;
nightgown, check; toothbrush, check.
We drive in silence.
I feel butterfly moths
turning around in my stomach,
imagining Aunt Birdie's garden
with the vines beginning to
creep up the trellis, the beautiful bright oranges of
trumpet vines
with soft yellow insides
outlining the center.

Mama takes a right on Livernois,
turns into the alley.
The stones pop under her tires.
"Mama, don't honk.
I want to surprise Aunt Birdie."
I get out slowly, make sure that
the Oldsmobile door doesn't squeak.
I stop, walk slowly…

A bee buzzes close, and Aunt Birdie
tries to swat it. I sneak up behind her,
hoping to surprise her as she quickly
slaps behind her neck to shoo away
the horse flies, and she smacks me instead.

"Ouch!" "Ah, my baby girl, Georgia. Well,
look at you! Only two weeks and you're shooting
up like a string bean." She squeezes
me so tight I can barely breathe.

"Let me look at you!"
"Mama's just parking in front.
She let me out in the back alley. I wanted to surprise
        you."

Mama brings in my overnight bag. Aunt Birdie's a nurse.
She works four days in long shifts, and she sells
Mary Kay cosmetics part-time.
Today will be gardening and Mary Kay deliveries,
and tomorrow roller-skating with Ceci.
Mama comes around back, gives Aunt Birdie
a big hug. I have my cue—they're going to
talk adult now.

Mama and Aunt Birdie talk,
me in the background in the lilacs
listening more to the bees than
Mama. I hear names—Ty, Jerome, my daddy—and
a bit about that strange man planting a
bowling ball. Mama plays down the lack
of welcome we've had in the neighborhood.

We've gone unnoticed or over-noticed.
Naomi's family has been nice but not really anyone else.
I let the bees in the lilacs tell me their stories as I sneak
to the front to open the mailbox to search for
the contest announcement.

The mailbox

There's a small cobweb wound 'round
the metal box. I blow it away, lift
the latch, reach inside, way down.
The metal scrapes my wrist I reach so
far. Nothing here today, nothing.

I race around to the back door
and come into the house.
"Auntie, when does your mail come?"
Mama looks at me like I'm a bit too nosy
and should stop where I started.
"Usually by noon. Why do you need to
know about my business, Georgia?
You're only spending the night, girl.
I hope you didn't forward your mailing
address for an overnight."
If she only knew.
I erase the guilty look I feel
creeping onto my face.

When Mama kisses me goodbye,
she and Auntie go out front, and I
find the mail on her marbled Formica
kitchen table by the napkins.
I'm careful as I pick it up,
leaf through one by one,
keeping the envelopes in the same order.
Just a bunch of bills today.
I place them back on the table,
just like I found them.

Roller skating with Ceci

The sun finally comes up
after my sleepless night.
It's finally time for Ceci to come.
I'm waiting on the stoop and
keep looking down the block.
I've cleaned up my skates and
have my skate key around my
neck. In the distance, I see Ceci. I can
tell by her walk and sway and then
I see right behind her—Wanda!

I wipe my eyes. Maybe it's another
neighborhood kid. No, it's her.
My chest feels tight, and my cheeks
get hot. This was not to be a
double date. Why does she think
I would want to see Wanda?
I'm taking deep breaths, slowly, so I
don't get dizzy. I feel my mad
creeping up all over me.

Ceci runs up to hug me.
I hug back. She's so in my face
and talking a mile a minute like she does.
She's acting like she hasn't
brought her sidekick, this Batman and

Robin duo. Wanda stands a bit to the side,
waves a small *hey*. Her skates are by
her side.
Aunt Birdie hugs both girls, as if they're
both my friends.

"Off you go, girls!"
Aunt Birdie waves us off to skate.
I'm glad that we are skating, since I don't
have to talk too much to either of them.

The pavement's welcoming and crooked
from the tree roots, not like the perfect pavement
of Southfield in front of Naomi's house,
with her handprint and Jax's paw molded in the cement.
We skate around the whole neighborhood
for hours. Past everything that makes
sense in my head.
Past everything I've been missing.
Past everything I know.

Blue flu

We're near Ceci's house,
but we can't come in. Her dad's a police officer
for the city, and his shift has changed to the night shift,
but Daddy told me the cops
are getting ready to strike soon.

The uneven pavement is starting to bother me,
or is it being in the middle of Ceci and Wanda?
I never thought she'd bring someone with her today.
Today...the day that I waited for,
for two weeks, Mama thinks.
It's really only one, since I went with
Jerome last week.

Lemonade and silence

We open the metal gate and stay on the
pavement by the house and take off our skates.
It's beginning to warm up, so I scoot over to
the grass, sit, and feel its coolness.

Aunt Birdie brings out a tray.
"Georgia, look! My famous lemonade!"
The glasses are beginning to sweat on the
table, forming little water pools by the bottom
that drip on me when I pick up the drink. It
feels cool as the water drips down my shirt.

Hopscotch

Ceci grabs some chalk and makes a hopscotch.
She and Wanda begin to play. They probably
expect me to move, but I feel like a goose lawn
ornament, stuck and frozen.

Aunt Birdie nudges me to take my turn,
but I just can't.
Ceci's being polite,
talking to me, and Wanda's bouncing
back and forth. I get up and play, but I feel
a wedge between us that makes this warm
day feel cold.

The longest visit

The day goes like this—
me being kinda there
and Ceci over-trying.
She and Wanda seem to have
too many inside jokes for two weeks.
I'm thinking about the poetry contest
and, hopefully, finding the envelope
before Aunt Birdie does.

"Do you know who won the contest?"
This stops them from walking down
their recent friendship memory lane.

"I don't know, but I do know that when I get to meet
Gwendolyn Brooks and be in her poetry book,
I will be famous…"
Ceci always thinks she knows everything.
"She's only acting as the judge,
and she's autographing the book…"
Ceci starts prancing around, all full of herself.
She races into the house and leaves Wanda with me.

Wanda tells me she sent in her poem too.
"My mama made me enter. I don't even like to write."
She leaves and follows Ceci.

Wanda shouldn't have even entered the contest.
I had been feeling better about her maybe being our
friend, but now she just seems in the way again.

Long before this contest was announced,
Mrs. Murphy always posted the best poems,
and mine were always on the bulletin board.

Cool colors

After they leave, I help Aunt Birdie sort the
cosmetic boxes, even though I don't
wear makeup yet... I love helping her
sort the orders. I go back to the inventory sheet
and read off nail polish colors like Cool Cream
and Red Roses and Pink Passion.
They sound like poems to me.
Mama's not interested in this stuff.
My mama's beautiful, but she says her beauty
stands on its own, and she is much more interested
in how people are on the inside than on the outside
and calls this nonsense.

Mama returns

Mama knocks on the door
and comes right in, kisses
me on my head, and asks how
my visit with Ceci was.
"Fine, Mama, but she brought that
Wanda with her. I thought she was coming alone."
"I'm sorry, baby."

"Birdie…" Mama calls by whistling to her
like she did when her sister was little.
She got her name by always pointing at the birds.
Grandmama and Pop Pop would point
to the bird and say, "Birdie," and my aunt would point
to herself and say, "Birdie." They would point to her
and say, "Bridget," and she would point to herself and
say, "Birdie," so it stuck.

Mama hangs out in the kitchen,
catching up on grown-up conversation.

Leaving now

Before I know it, it is time to go.
I give Aunt Birdie a hug and don't
let go. "Mama, when will we come back?"
"Don't worry. It won't be too long."
I'm not sure I can hug without crying.
"Birdie, come by our house for
dinner next Wednesday to see the new house."
Aunt Birdie works four days on and three days off
at the hospital.
"Sure will."
Kisses are shared and then we go.

Back here

When we get back, I do not want
to go into the house with Mama.
I look down the street to see
if Naomi and her grandpa are
around. I am hoping not…

I walk up to the bowling ball
on the lawn. The sun's shining
on it, making it look like marble.
I lean down, make sure that no one
is watching me. I touch the smooth
surface. It's heated from the midday sun.
I try to move it, even though I know it's
immovable. This object that is
usually in motion is still.
It is now permanently planted and I wonder how,
and if I will ever be…

I run upstairs to my cool, air-conditioned
room, bury my head in my pillow.
Tears start. I feel my journal and, between
the blur in my eyes, I write.

How to lose a friend

Watch your best friend
replace you with her new
best friend.

Watch her act like it's fun
and okay all day.

Get mad and wish that you had
never moved and that everything
stayed the same.

Sunday, July 2

Tree watering

I sleep in late, don't want to
get up, still feel bad about
Ceci. I need to do something.
I go downstairs and look out the
front window.

The tree's leaves are looking
wilted.
It has been so dry that the dirt
takes the water in quickly.

I'm in pj's, but I don't care.
I walk out, hope no one sees me.

I get out the hose and gently
start to soak the tree. The water
slowly creeps into the dirt,
the roots thankful.
I hear Miss Brooks's poem "Tommy,"
about planting seeds and watering them.

The tree manual said
transplanting shouldn't be done
in summer, better in fall when
growth season slows down.
Daddy told Jerome that this would be his job,

but I'm worried the tree won't survive.
It never should've been dug up
and moved.
We should've stayed too.

The TV war

Daddy's staring at the TV.
It's the news with the war on TV.
Daddy gets up,
turns the volume down.
He never wants me to hear the newscaster
and get upset.

"Hi, baby. How was your visit yesterday?"
I give him a hug and start to tell
him about Wanda, but I can see
he's preoccupied with the news.
"Go help your mama set the table
for breakfast."

I walk toward the kitchen and stay
in the dining room, silently watching
the TV screen. He doesn't know that I always
watch from here when the news is
on. I look for Ty every time.
It's worse when I can't hear
what they are saying as I watch
children run with clothes on fire
and no words.

A note on the desk

As I am setting the table
I see another letter from Vietnam.
I don't want to wait until later
for all of us to read it. Daddy's
already opened it. I grab it, sneak
into the bathroom, and begin to read.

I turn on the bathroom fan
so no one can hear the crinkle
of the paper.
Ty says he would send pictures
soon and that he has a surprise.
My birthday's coming soon,
so maybe that's what he is talking
about.

Dear Daddy, Mama, Jerome, and Little Bit,

I received your last letter telling me about the new house.
I hope that I can see it soon, but I do not know when that will be.
I am sending Georgia a birthday postcard. Happy birthday, Little
Bit!
I copied from your favorite poet Gwendolyn Brooks.
She wrote this when she was thirteen.
It's called "Eventide."

I begin to read it. The words wrap
around me like a soft blanket. The last
line holds me close and gives me hope,

telling me that my worries will go away.

Inside the envelope a picture drops out.

Ty and his friends look long and scraggly.
They're smoking cigarettes.
I've seen enough of that on TV.
Ty's 'fro is out to the side.

Ty doesn't look like himself
or like his senior picture when he
was so clean-cut.

"Georgia, where are you? Daddy
asked you to set the table!"
"Coming, Mama…"
I flush to cover my tracks and
carefully place the letter back on
the desk, the same way I found it.

Poem to Ty

Before bed, images of Ty
swirl in my head.
I get out
my journal.

How to miss your brother

Be sad that Ty can't ever go
back to our old house.

Be frustrated that Daddy is
trying to keep you from seeing
the news.

Feel a loss when you
send a letter, never knowing
if Ty will read it.

Feel crazy, wondering when and if
he will be coming back.

Monday, July 3

Monday day off holiday

Naomi's coming up the sidewalk.
I race downstairs.
She has her bike, and she tells me
to hop on.
"Mama, I'm going with Naomi."
I walk down the street to get on the bike.
I'm not sure where we're going.

We go past all the houses.
There's an empty overgrown lot.
We hop off the bike. She ditches
it to the side. We walk through stick-tights,
field daisies, and thick branches that scratch me.
There's an old couch, half a table, and
a bucket.

The white butterfly moths circle in the air,
twirling around each other. The sun's shining
through the leaves.

I am thinking that I need to tell someone
about the contest. I can't tell Ceci—who knows?—
she might tell Wanda. Jerome's always busy with
baseball, and Ty's away.

We sit on an old wooden plank

that's balancing on an old tree branch.

"Have you ever wanted anything so bad that
it's all you ever think about day and night?"

"Yep, all the time when I'm watching the Tigers.
I keep imagining myself going to the game
with my daddy. Mom says I shouldn't hold my
breath for that."

I'm not sure that I should say anything,
but I can't keep this to myself any longer.

"Naomi, can I trust you to keep a secret?
You can't tell anyone about this, not even Jerome."

I take a deep breath and begin.
"I entered a poetry contest."

"Hey, good luck with that, Emily Dickinson…"
It doesn't seem like Naomi would know about poetry.

"No, not like that. She's okay, but she's not my favorite.
Seriously, I entered the Spirit of Detroit Poetry Contest
for kids going into fourth through seventh grade who
    live in Detroit.
It's a really big deal!
The winner's poem gets painted on a building."

"Okay, really, good luck…"

"It's not about luck, it's about lying…"

"Lying about what?"

"You have to live in Detroit to win."

"Who's gonna know? You might not even win."

"Thanks! I lied and used Aunt Birdie's address in Detroit,
and since we moved, I'll probably be disqualified."

"Your secret is safe with me. I think everybody does that
kind of thing once and awhile. I'm sure you're fine.
Don't worry…"

"Speaking of secrets, let's play hide-and-seek."
I'm not sure if I made a mistake by telling her, but I let
        it go
and play. I just hope she doesn't tell Jerome.

I've found three great hiding spots.
My last one is in the tree.
A rock hits me from the side.
It stings.
I grab my arm and feel a bit of blood trickle down.
I look around, but I can't see Naomi.
I know it's not her, even joking.
I see two kids running fast. It looks like Joey's hair
from behind. I see Naomi take off after Joey and Scott.
I see Joey throw the first punch at Naomi, but Naomi
is fast ,and she trips him from behind and knocks him
down. Naomi has him down, and she is sitting on his
belly and punches him right in the nose. It doesn't take
        long till
she gets it right, and his nose starts bleeding. Scott

peels Naomi off Joey and tells her to leave him alone.

"I'm gonna tell Jerome about this, Joey. Maybe he'll
kick you off the team!"
"Kick me off the team?
Who just gave me a bloody nose?"
Scott spits on the ground to look tough.

It all happens so fast; I don't know what to
think. Joey seems so angry all the time, but he's no match
for Naomi.

Deeper trouble than the contest lie

I'm thrilled and scared at the same time.
If Daddy finds out about this,
he won't let me hang out with Naomi,
and she's all I've got here now.

Daddy will remind me:
"Georgia, we Johnsons only need good reasons to stand
    out."
His list is strong in my head.
We Johnsons want to stand out for the right reasons
and then he begins the list:
"Your brother is decorated in Vietnam.
Jerome made varsity.
Your mama's honored at the college, and I got a
    promotion
at the city planning office." And then the speech:
"I expect to see the best from you, Georgia Johnson.
I expect you to shine!"

I look up at the sky, as if there's a star to wish on
in the hot midday sun.
Even though it's a star, it's not
the wishing kind.
I close my eyes tight,
crossing my fingers, hoping this will go away
and my daddy won't hear about the fight.
He used to like to watch Ali fight but thinks
he's a coward now.

But I don't even want to know how he
would ground me for this.
I can't stand it any longer. I need to tell someone
in my family. I trust Ty.

Tuesday, July 4

My thirteenth birthday

Mama's off work today. Almost
everyone else has the day off too.
It's a national holiday, my birthday, July Fourth.
Ceci and a family friend, Jackie, are coming
for the day, and Ceci is sleeping over tonight.

I've spent days trying to figure out if I should invite
    Naomi.
She's just so different than Ceci, but I don't want to
    leave her out.
I can always say that Jerome's coaching her if it gets too
    weird.
I don't think she'll want to talk girl-talk or microphone
lip-sync
to my records, and Ceci won't
really want to hear about baseball.

The doorbell rings and I run to get it.
Mama's promised to take us to the Southfield Parks
and Rec pool, since I haven't been there yet.
We go upstairs to listen to records until
Mama's ready to go. She hands me three swim
caps, all with funny, bright orange and pink floppy
    flowers on them.
I'm sure Naomi won't wear one.

I put on Martha and the Vandellas

"Dancing in the Streets."
Ceci always gets to be Martha.
Jackie and I will be back-up,
our hips swaying.
We use our special hand movements.
We always used to argue about who would get to be
Martha,
but Ceci's got a better voice than me,
so I don't argue now.

After a few songs, I hear Mama shouting
to get ready—Naomi's here.
Naomi has her T-shirt and shorts on, and I'm wondering
if she even has a swimsuit.
She lifts up her shirt. "Yup, I got it," she says, as if she
    read my mind.
"Hey," she says before I can introduce her.
She's got her Tigers hat on and her ponytail tied up
in back. Jerome comes down and grabs her hat, and they
begin to chase around the house like cats and dogs until
Mama yells, "Jerome, give it back!"
"Ceci and Jackie, this is Naomi." They shyly wave.
Out-of-breath, Naomi says, "Hey."

We get in the back of Mama's blue Ford Galaxie.
I sit up front with Mama but keep looking back
to see how they're getting along.
We're not used to having to take a car to the pool.
Back home, each neighborhood had a park and a pool
every twelve blocks or so.
Things in the suburbs are spread out like a flat prairie,
looking all the same—lots of empty fields with weeds,
where houses are not.

Southfield Pool

Mama drops us in front, and we get out.
She tells us to wait till she parks.
I'm sure I don't want to get out without her.

Ceci, Jackie, and my mom and I are the only Black people
    here.
I'm not sure this was such a good plan.
What were she and Daddy thinking?

My stomach gets that gnawing feeling, like
when you haven't eaten,
but I don't need to eat.
The woman at the ticket counter asks how
many residents and nonresidents.
"Three residents and one visitor, please."
The woman gives Mama a look, as if to question her.
"How many residents?" the lady repeats.
Mama raises her left eyebrow—her you-better-
get-serious-or-I-will face. The woman takes
her money and then lets her know that we can get our
pictures taken for ID cards, which will be
sent in the mail.
This will be pretty cool, I think, like a license picture.
Mama mutters under her breath,
"I guess this lady's welcoming us to the neighborhood."

Mama's keeping her cool better than I thought.
This must be my first birthday gift. We go and lay
out our towels on the beach chairs and ask Mama

if we can go right in the water.
Mama's brought her book. She usually
reads mysteries, but it looks like she's grabbed a
light romance. She's trying to hang out,
get away from her professor work for a bit.

Ceci and Naomi head to the diving boards.
Jackie and me stay together.
"No, go ahead. We're fine," I say.
I'm too much of a coward for the diving board.
I slide into the shallow end slowly.
It's hot out, but the water is really cold.
They jump right in. I go piece by piece, till I'm all wet.

A short break and a problem

The lifeguard blows the whistle for a break.
It's adult swim. Mama gives us some money for a
snack. We run up ahead, and then I slow down.
I see Joey from down the street. I don't
like him at all. I don't know what he'll say or do.
"Hurry up, Georgia, the line's gonna be long," Naomi
    prods.
"I don't want to be near that Joey kid."
"He probably doesn't remember you."

I get to the counter, order hot dogs, fries, and
    cherry slushies.
Ceci and Naomi get the same.
"Let's fix these dogs up," Naomi says.
Ceci and Naomi go up to the counter, and Joey's
there. I see it before it happens—his foot slips
out and trips Ceci. I try to get there to stop
her fall, catch her food, but it's too late.
I help her up and get her to a bench, and then
I don't even think.

I run over, but Naomi beats me to it.
We both start yelling at him
until one of the park's people comes over
and stops us.

I know I've made a big mistake,
but I can't stand this type of kid.
"Ceci, are you all right?"

She brushes it off.
"I must have tripped on that table leg."
"Or somebody's leg."
I look over at Joey accusingly.

By this time a small crowd
has gathered around. I am hoping
that Mama is so into her book that
she won't see us with the park's people
all around us.

"What is the matter with you?" I hiss at Joey,
feeling all of my new thirteen years.
"Why'd you trip her?"
He looks as if I am talking a different language.
The park's people tell us that we'll get a warning
this time, but if it happens again, they will
have to contact our parents.

For the rest of the swim time, we decide
to play a tag game and then do handstands
and cartwheels in the pool.

Ice cream instead of cake

Instead of a birthday cake this year, Mama
decides to go to Farrell's Ice Cream Parlor.
I beg her to not take me to the place where
they make you wear a hat and sing to you.
I really don't want to be noticed this way.
We did that last year for Ceci's birthday
and shared a gigantic sundae for three.
It was called the Pig Trough.

"You can have two scoops today, Georgia,"
Mama says. I feel guilty for having one
since what happened at the pool,
but Joey had it coming to him.
I hope that Mama doesn't find out.

"Caramel sundae, two scoops, please."
This birthday is working out all right,
and Naomi is just being good ol' Naomi.
Just hanging out. We sit in a booth
and they start to sing "Happy Birthday"
to me, and I still duck under the table.

The sleepover

When we get back, Naomi walks home,
and Jackie's parents come by.

Daddy's bringing home Chinese food from How Kow,
my favorite—vegetable fried rice and chopsticks.
Plus, I get an extra wish, a fortune cookie wish.
When we finish I get to open the
first fortune cookie, then my gifts are
in the living room. I have already picked
them up and shaken them.
One is really flat and another
one really small.

My birthday fortune is: *It's never
too late to learn.* A bit preachy since
the mistake I made at the pool,
but I'll take it.
Ceci's says, *Enjoy the luck that a companion brings you.*
She smiles the smile she had back in Mrs. Murphy's class.

No dessert tonight since we just had
ice cream, so we set dishes aside
so I can get to my presents.
I know it's a record, a 45,
but I don't know who it is.
I carefully tear each corner till everyone's saying,
"Georgia, just rip it off."
"Daddy, thank you! Ceci, look!"
We both squeal.

"Ain't No Mountain High Enough."

We jump up, get out our hand-microphones,
and start singing, and then, in the middle, sing out loudly.
We are swaying and switchin', moving our hands
and laughing out loud, and I know the old Ceci
is back. We fall to the ground laughing.

"Now, baby, follow me to the garage."
Mama tells me to put my hands over
my eyes. She leads me carefully into the
dark garage and opens the automatic door.
One side is her car and, for some
reason, Daddy's car is out front.
The sun shines into the garage, and
I see why. In his spot where his car should
be is a perfect bright yellow
banana-seat bike.
A banana seat that looks like a banana—
that's the cool part.
The uncool part is that there's this
gigantic orange flagpole coming out
the back of it. I look at Mama with
pleading eyes.
"Daddy just wants you to be safe."
I hug them both hard and feel some
of the anger start to gently fade away,
for today.

Ceci hops on the back, and we get
ready to ride around the block double.
Mama eyes me.
"Just this one time, Georgia."

Even though it's July Fourth

Even though it's July Fourth,
the weather doesn't care.
Fireworks canceled tonight…
The rain comes down.
There've been so many ups
and downs today, I can't
keep track, so we go upstairs
and listen to thunder
instead of fireworks.

Popcorn and secrets

I think I should tell Ceci about the lie.
I know I can trust her.
Mama knocks on the door,
brings us popcorn in my grandma's red fiesta bowl.
When her footsteps have safely passed, I tell Ceci,
"I have a secret to tell you."
The words feel stuck in my throat.
"I entered the Spirit of Detroit Poetry Contest."
"I know. So did I."
"You don't understand. I wrote down my aunt's
address because I knew you had to live in Detroit
to enter."
"Georgia, you know you
could be disqualified if anyone finds out."
Her voice is full of telling me off.
"Ceci, you better pinky swear right now
that you will never tell a soul."
We put out our pinkies and hold them
tight, until it hurts.
I'm not sure if it's too much ice cream,
popcorn, or birthday, but my stomach
is starting to turn.

Fireworks rained out

"Ceci, maybe I can come back and
see the fireworks at the Detroit River
with you tomorrow night.
You know they always do two nights.
Remember last summer when I would
sleep at your house, and then we would
sleep at mine, and we would go back and
forth and back and forth, and we started
leaving our stuff at each other's houses?
I can ask Mama if—"

"Georgia…"
She interrupts me.
"I already promised
Wanda that I would go
on the Fifth with her."

I try to act cool with it.
"Oh yeah, sure…"
I wonder, Can I still be jealous?
And is she even a bit jealous
about Naomi?

Wednesday morning back at camp and a reason to leave

When we arrive back at camp on Wednesday
there's this guy there with long, curly hair, a beard,
and a tie-dyed T-shirt. Misty's acting a bit
different and seems to have stars in her eyes.

Every once in a while, he places his hand on
Misty's shoulder, and she gives him a look.
"Girls, this is Josh and he's going to help
out today. He's from Ann Arbor, where
he's at the university studying poli-sci."
Naomi looks over to me and mouths, *Poli-sci?*
I nudge her in the ribs and whisper to the side,
"Political science." I've known all the abbreviations
since I was younger, looking at Mama's course book
when I was learning to read. I would sound out each
abbreviation as if it was a new word.

With Josh helping out, I decide that we can
sneak back to Detroit today. Misty won't need
us, and Naomi doesn't have practice today.
The heat index is going to be up to 100 and the
city called off all games. We got the call
early this morning, so Jerome was still hanging
out in bed when I walked over to camp.

Misty is getting all excited to teach everyone
songs and put on a play before summer is
over. Josh gets out his guitar. He's teaching
the little kids "We all live in a yellow submarine."

There are too many words in the verses, but
the kids all chime in on the "yellow submarine"
part. While he's singing with the kids, Misty
has us setting up large white paper so that
the kids can paint a yellow submarine.
We set up paintbrushes for the kids
and big white T-shirts.

While we set up, I tell Naomi that
I want to go back to Detroit to see if the contest
envelope has arrived. It's a great day
to go, since Misty will be wrapped up
with Josh all day. I brought my purse
today, so we can leave right from Kennedy.

Looking for the contest envelope

I have told my brother
that I am going to Naomi's house after camp,
and she's told her grandpa
that she is going to my house after camp.
Tracks covered…
I'm getting too good at this lying thing.

We meet at the corner of the block,
head toward the Mobile station.
The large winged horse is lit up, even
in the daytime. I'm hanging around
the garage door. I ask the mechanic
about the bus schedules.
From under the car, he motions
his grease-covered arm toward the station.
The schedules are by the cigarette counter.
I grab a schedule while I keep
looking at the cigarettes above the counter.
Naomi looks like she's going to try to take
 a pack of cigarettes but asks instead.

She says her dad's in the car and points
to the Mercury Ford Monarch that
was by the pump when we walked up.
She whispers to me that she buys cigarettes
for her dad all the time.

Change

I think we will be in enough trouble...
She hands the guy a dollar for a twenty-seven cent
pack and gets the change for the bus fare. I'm already
outside the station, not wanting to be a part of this.
We go over to the bus bench and wait. I'm kinda mad,
not wanting to talk to her, but I need her not to be mad
at me now.

I poke her with my sharp elbow.
"What are you doing?"
"Feeling groovy," she sings.
"Mom never let Dad smoke in the house,
but that's not the reason he left.
My mom doesn't have too many rules...
They didn't even seem to argue, and they never really
    talked."

The bus

The bus squeals as it pulls to the curb
and stops.
I walk onto the bus with confidence.
Ty and Jerome took me on the bus all the time.
Now I'm acting like I do it every day of the week myself.
"Come on, Naomi..."
I walk her past the first few seats and we settle in.
I am feeling butterflies rolling in my stomach.
I am beside myself excited to see Aunt Birdie.
I want to surprise her, so I didn't call.

I look at the stops and try to figure out
how many. We'll take this bus down
Greenfield to 8 Mile.
We are getting stares after a few minutes.
Heads are turning slightly, and some people humming.
I am not sure if it's because we're kids alone
or because Naomi's white.

8 Mile

We pass under the 8 Mile viaduct, hear
the *whoosh* overhead and the *thump-bump* as we cross
between Southfield and Detroit.
I figure it's about eight stops in all.
First under the bridge, Starlight Motel
with the neon shooting stars, Jack in the Box restaurant,
Marathon gas station, Cunningham Drugstore,
and then the Strike King Bowling Alley.
I feel Naomi tugging my arm,
and she pulls the wire for the bus to stop.
I try to grab her arm and end up falling into
her lap.
"What're you doing?" I am short with her,
feeling impatient.
"I gotta go—"
"Geez, we don't have time."
I'm getting mad at her, but the bus has already stopped...
"I gotta pee really bad—" Naomi says, jumping up and
    down.
I'm beginning to feel this is a mistake to have had Naomi
    come at all.

I've been to the bowling alley before.
Ty's girlfriend's mama is the bartender here.
I don't want to go in and don't want to stay out.
I go into the hallway.
"This won't take long, pinky swear."
"What if anyone sees us?" Naomi starts sneaking along
    like Agent 86

in *Get Smart*.
I guess I'd rather be Agent 99, since she's
quieter and figures things out.
I am wishing that Naomi was more like Ceci than she is.

Shirley, the bartender, is at the bar,
but I'm trying to be quiet, not be noticed.
She might be mad that Ty broke up with her daughter
when he left for Vietnam.
She spots Naomi as she exits the bathroom.
"Hey, Nome, a few days early?"
Naomi's face turns red, and she stammers, like
she doesn't have a snappy comeback.
"Grandpa's coming later. He dropped me off."

She grabs my arm, and we run out,
catching our breath by the side of the building.
The next bus breezes past. Our transfer tickets
fly out of our hands and into the street. We'll be walking
the rest if we want to take the bus home.
We won't have enough for a new bus ticket.
I'm hoping that Shirley doesn't come out to help
Naomi's grandpa, and we get caught.
It's easier hanging at the school.
Why'd I think this would be fine? Self-doubt starts
creeping up me like Aunt Birdie's trellis of trumpet vines.

The approach

We walk in silence. I only hear the flap
of Naomi's wooden Dr. Scholl's against
the soles of her feet.
We arrive by the back alley, where lilac's blooming like
sweet perfume. It smells fake.
I see the steel-blue lawn chair
in the backyard, fresh grass
clippings on the lawn.
We walk to the front and
knock. No answer.

I check the mailbox.
Some of the rusty metal shreds in my hand.
No contest letter, only bills. I use some of the rust to
draw a small heart on the envelope and then a *G*.
"Damn..." My eyes are welling up.
It's too hot, and I'm too tired.
If Mama or Aunt Birdie heard
me say that word, I would know why I
don't.

The deli

We walk into Weiss's Deli.
The screen door clips my heel.
The coolness of the refrigerator case feels
good as sweat drips down,
warmth blows from the blower
onto our feet.

I look at the cow tongue in the case, blue veins.
The dried white fish stares back at us, one glazed
eye open. On the counter is a huge glass container
with gigantic pickles inside.
Aunt Birdie stores these in her basement for Mr. Weiss.

"My grandpa eats tongue. I won't go near it," Naomi says,
with her hands in her pockets.
The dried white fish is staring back at us.

Mr. Weiss comes around and wipes
meat-covered hands on his white apron.
"How's my Georgia, the house?"
I hug him back hard, getting my fingers tangled in his
    apron strings.
"Have you seen Aunt Birdie?"
"Vat? You think I am a magician and can know
    everything?"
He has a thick accent but
I have known him my whole life
so I can understand him.

We tell him we need to go.

"Please don't tell Aunt Birdie."

His look tells me he doesn't approve, but will do it
     anyways.

"Vait, I'll give you girls some rye bread heels."

"Thanks!" we both shout, racing down the street.

We hop on the bus, take a transfer, and hope
we get back before our parents find out.

A surprise guest

At dinner, Mama asks about my day and tells me
Aunt Birdie is coming tonight, since she worked on
my birthday.
I tell her about the camp.
"In the afternoon, I was with Naomi, outside."
It's not quite the truth, and it's not quite a lie.
I'm getting too good at this lying thing.
Before I wrote Aunt Birdie's address,
I didn't even know how to lie,
not like the lie I started on the last day of school.

A happy thought.
Aunt Birdie comes tonight
for dinner, for the first time
in the new house,
and she will never know
that we were at her house today.

Backyard grill

I smell the charcoal for the grill.
Mama told Daddy to keep it simple.
We're just having hamburgers and hot dogs,
and Aunt Birdie's bringing potato salad.
Mama didn't want to mess with a big
dinner in the beginning of the week.

Aunt Birdie visits

Mama's picked up Aunt Birdie right
from work at the hospital, so she still has her
smock on. She works with the kids, so she
always has fun prints. She's brought her
clothes to change into and relax.
I can barely wait for her to change
since I am the Official Tour Guide.

I show her room to room in our new house as I hold her
hand. She sounds impressed.
Mama has asked me to make iced tea
and lemonade, so I get started.

Each time we start talking about something,
I keep thinking about telling her about
the mailbox, but no time seems like
a good time. We are having such a
nice visit. I don't want to ruin it.

Before she leaves, I hug her hard,
inhale all that is my auntie,
wonder if she can tell that we were at her house today.

After she leaves I need to rest

I'm getting too good at lying.
I get out my journal and write.

How to Lie

Simple.
Tell the lie to yourself enough times
that you begin to believe it,
or at least for twenty-one days,
you might talk yourself into it...

New builts after camp

Naomi has practice on the back
field today but told me that in
the afternoon she wants to take
me somewhere.

We ride down Mt. Vernon Street,
which is mostly gravel; they are starting to put
tar on one side of the road.
The sweet smell of it and the heat
make me feel dizzy.
I can see the warped waves
rising on the pavement.

We get off the bike. There's
a lot of dirt and the frame of a house.
It's a construction site.
"Should we be here?" I ask her quietly,
as if the sky might open and hear us.

She acts like she doesn't hear me.
"They're my dad's houses. I used to
be here with him all the time.
There are plywood planks and
cardboard to walk on and a big
gap where the stairs would be.

Watch where you walk—there
are nails everywhere."

We walk carefully up the steps
to the invisible upstairs. The floorboards
are covered with pinkish-brown paper.
We both lie down and look up at the
clouds.

"That one to the left is definitely a seahorse."

"Hey, to the right of that it looks like a fish.
See the tail? It reminds me of one of the stamps
on Ty's letters, my brother. I told you
he's in Vietnam."
"A dog."
"A dragon"

We go on like this for a long time.
It becomes peacefully silent as we let the
hot sun warm us on this cloudy day.

Needing to be more careful

I'm walking carefully. Then I hear it.
"Ouch!" Naomi's sitting down, grabbing
her foot. I know what's happened.
The nail's gone right through the
rubber sole of her Keds sneakers.

She's trying not to cry, but it's no use.
I run over, take a look, don't want
to do what I know I need to do.
"Naomi, I'm going to pull it out. Turn the
other way." I'm careful the way that
I grab it and pull it out. Aunt Birdie taught me
well. Naomi winces, tears coming down slowly.

I know I will need to take her home,
put some mercurochrome on it,
make sure that we don't tell anyone.
Naomi leans on my shoulder, hops
careful and slow. She's holding
on. It's going to be hard to lie about this.
I'm getting too good at thinking about new lies.

We get back to her house. Grandpa Herman's
napping in the front room. We sneak
down the hall to the bathroom.

I get a cotton ball and clean Noami's foot.
"Youch! Why'd you have to do that?"
"Shush! You'll wake up your grandpa,
and then you'll have a lot of explaining to do."

One more try:

Now that I've seen Aunt Birdie,
I feel even guiltier.
I want to go back and check
the mailbox. We'll wait until
late afternoon when Aunt Birdie's
out of the house.

I go out to the field.
Naomi's up to bat, and Jerome's
pitching. He's been feeling a bit
better about being here because
he met with the high school coach,
and the team's actually short several players,
since some kids are moving.

I think that one of them is Joey's older
brother, so I'll be happy he's moving.
Goodbye, good riddance.
I can't believe it. I never
saw a *For Sale* sign down the street.

Jerome doesn't care; he just wants to play
varsity ball, so he's happy. He wants to
play pro and get scouted by colleges.
Mama and Daddy say he needs to think
about both college and ball.

I wait until Jerome and Naomi
are finished putting things away.

Jerome smacks Naomi on the head,
and she smacks him back. I think
she's the little sister he should have
ordered. I think he misses hanging out and
playing with Ty. He likes me well enough
though. "Michael from the team is coming
over today to shoot some hoops, so both of
you need to be outta the way, okay?"

Perfect. I ask Naomi to hang back.
"You want to go back to Detroit on the bus?"
We grab quick peanut butter sandwiches and
take her blue banana seat. It will be much easier
to lock up her blue bike, and mine stands out
like the setting sun.
We lock and hide the bike
behind the gas station. I send in Naomi to get
our tickets, and we're off.

In Aunt Birdie's mailbox

We know the route now, passing the familiar
stops. Naomi pulls down the bus wire. *Ding!*
We hop off. I act like Agent 007 and sneak
around the back and whistle Aunt Birdie's and
my whistle, and wait.
"The coast is clear!"

I reach into the mailbox.
My sweaty hand sticks to the flier,
Hudson's department store fall editions.
I find an envelope that says *City of Detroit*,
and my heart skips. I read further, see
the light bulb of the Detroit Edison bill.

I put it back in, and there's one more envelope
lying tightly against the box.
The return address says *City of Detroit*.
I see an embossed picture of the
Spirit of Detroit Statue and the words
The Spirit of Detroit Poetry Contest.
I feel excited and nervous at the same time.
Now I'm not sure I want to find out. I hand it to Naomi.
"Open it!"
"No wait…I need to sit down!"
"Okay, now."
Do I cross my fingers? Not cross?
Stand, so I can jump up and down?
Sit, so I can be sitting if it's nothing?
"Georgia…"

"Okay, I'm ready."

Dear Georgia Johnson,

*Congratulations! You are a finalist in the Spirit of Detroit Poetry
Contest. As a finalist, we invite you to the Detroit Public Library
on Thursday, July 13th. You may bring one invited guest.
Location: 5201 Woodward Avenue, Detroit Michigan, 48202*

Sincerely,

Dudley Randall

"Wahoooo! I'm so excited I'm going to tell
Mama and…"
I calm down, realize that I can't tell
her. I feel happy and ashamed all
at the same time.
Naomi and Ceci hold this secret now.

I'm worried that maybe I should write
a letter, tell them where I live, come clean,
but the whole lie keeps getting deeper the longer
I wait.

"It says I can only take one person.
Let's go to Ceci's and tell her
the good news!"
We run down my auntie's street and then
turn the corner.

I come around the block, letter in hand,
and who should be sitting there

but Ceci and Wanda!
I look back, see that Naomi hasn't
kept up with me. She looks
hot and tired.
I hold up my envelope and see that Ceci's
holding one also.
I get excited and ask, "Are you also a finalist?"
"No…"
"Then why are you holding the envelope?"
"It's Wanda's."
I get that burning feeling in my eyes.
My words get caught in my throat.
"Ceci, but you'll still come with me, right?"
"Sorry, Georgia, but Wanda just asked and I said
yes."
"Well, unsay it!" I stomp away.
I'm so mad I can't believe it.

It's awfully quiet now, like a silent snowy day
when snowflakes fall, but this is a thick quiet,
like melting-tar-on-a-hot-summer-day kind
of quiet.

Why'd she choose her?

I turn around, walk away, the excited feelings
gone. "Okay, see you around…"
I can't believe Ceci's going with Wanda.
I forget that Naomi's still there.
Shoot, now I've done it…
"Naomi, you okay?"
Now I realize I've hurt Naomi's feelings.
Naomi pulls her hat
farther down than usual.

Naomi and I walk back in silence as we
make our way to catch the bus.

We see the bus; we're on time.
Steam rises from the manhole
and adds to the hot day.
We sit sideways in our quiet.

I'm not sure if I should ask Naomi
to go with me. I decide to ask.
"Thanks for coming with me today.
Do you want to come with me
next week to the ceremony?"
"No, no, that's okay. I think I have a
game that day anyways. We're heading toward playoffs."
I've never seen Naomi look like this.
I'm not sure how to undo what I did.

The rest of the ride is uncomfortable and hot.
The envelope is in my hand and is curling from
the moisture. If everything was the truth,
I'd run home to Mama and tell her the good news.
But the good news is quiet news.
I wish I could go home and tell Mama,
but it's my lie.

We get off the bus,
unlock Naomi's bike and ride back together.
I try to make her feel better.
"Do you want to go to Efros and get some gum?"
"No, I'm good." We ride in a hot-wind silence.

At home

When I get back, I run upstairs, place
the letter in my sock drawer. I take it out again.
It feels so good and bad at the same time.
"Georgia, you feeling okay?" asks Jerome.
"I'm just tired."
Jerome looks up
and gives me that
I'm-not-sure-what-you've-been-up-to look.

I need to let Ty know.
I can't deal with the secret much longer…

Dear Ty,

I need to tell you this because I
lied, but please, please,
please do not tell Mama and Daddy.
It's good news and its bad news.
I am a finalist in the
Spirit of Detroit Poetry Contest,
and I know you would be proud
of me.
I wasn't thinking, and it's
not like me…
You have to live
in Detroit to enter.
I read the rules and used Aunt Birdie's
Detroit address, and then we moved.
I did it anyways.

I did it because it's not
fair that we had to move.
If my poem doesn't win, it won't matter.
Please don't tell Mama and Daddy…

Love Georgia,

Yours,
Little Bit who told One Big Lie…

I wrap the letter up in two
envelopes, even though
Mama and Daddy will say,
No, it will cost too much to
send overseas.

I wrap it up so they
won't see. I wrap it
up to hide. I wrap it up
so my lie will disappear.

Friday, July 7

In the afternoon

It's like a duel—both of us trying to decide who
will stay at camp or who will go. Naomi leaves first but
I don't want it to look like I'm copying or chasing her,
so I let her go.

I hang out after lunch awhile and help Misty
with the young kids' bathing suits and sprinklers.
She decides it would be fun to put paint on their
feet and have them walk across a large piece of
    butcher paper.
They line up like ducks, following their mama.

I come home, grab lunch. I don't want to
talk to Ceci. I want to talk to Naomi,
but she doesn't want to talk to me.

I go for a bike ride on my yellow banana seat with my
orange flag. I ride quickly past Joey's house.
I want to avoid his house as much as possible.
I look to the side and don't see him, and then just
as I pass his house, he rides up on his bike and
I crash right into him.
"Hey, look out!" He skids past and says,
"It's because of you that we have to move."

His words sting worse than the scrape.

I am still righting my bike when I see Naomi's
grandpa come over to see if I'm okay.
"Thank you. I wasn't paying attention."
"Naomi's waiting for her dad to come and pick her
up. She thinks he might have Tigers tickets, but
I think she might be waiting on the porch for a long
    time."

I wave sheepishly as I pass by. Naomi tips her Tigers hat.
I go in and clean up my cut and figure out what I'm going
to wear to the library next week.

Mama spills the beans

"Baby, what happened?"
"That Joey's so mean. I accidentally
sideswiped him on my bike. He got all
upset and said he had to move because of me."

Mama's face drops from her usual smile.
"Oh, baby, I'm so sorry. Someone's always
gonna be first to make a change. Baby, some
people are just filled with hate. Daddy and I
knew this would be tough, but we couldn't
let what happened to Ty happen to Jerome."

I'm not sure what she's saying.

Now we are both beginning to cry. Mama doesn't
usually break down this way, but this has pushed her
too far.

"I guess I haven't been fair keeping this from you.
You really are old enough to hear the reason we moved."

It's one of those things that when you are wanting
    something
for so long, and you know it will never come,
    you let it go.
Now, I'm not even sure that I want to know the reason.
Mama pulls me closer and starts telling me
why we moved.

"Maybe I was afraid if I said it, it would make it more
true.

The Army recruiters always set up a table
at the high school lobby to enlist the young boys.
They tell them about how when they're done serving,
the Army will pay for their education.
There's still a draft, but they are always looking for kids.
If Jerome goes to college, he might not be drafted either.

"Ty had that Army brochure in his book bag for weeks.
I'd keep seeing it on his bedside table, and I'd throw it
        out,
and then another one would appear. He was just
waiting to turn eighteen to join. He wanted so much to
be like his uncle Russell. He was so proud of him."
Her voice begins to crack.

"Ty never even talked to us about it…
until he had signed up.
He was eighteen. He could decide; we couldn't
stop him. Ty did it on his own, but
Jerome's got good friends joining this year too.
I can't let him go…"

I decide not to tell Mama about the brochure
or the missing envelope.

I am beginning to understand why we moved
in Jerome's senior year. I grab Mama tight and
hug her hard. I tell her,
"It will be all right,
Mama, you'll see."
Mama tells me to go get
cleaned up for dinner.
"Baby, stay away from
that house until they're all moved."

Naomi waits

Most of the night I'm upstairs listening to my
records. I hear Jax barking and look outside.
Naomi's still sitting on the porch when the car
pulls up as the sun is setting a perfect pink hue.

Jax runs up to Naomi's dad and gives him a lick.
The garage's open, and I notice that her mom
is nowhere to be seen. Every once in a while,
I look outside to see if her dad's still there. They
are playing catch in the backyard until the stars
come out. I'm happy for Naomi.
Her dad is finally there.

Saturday, July 8

Early morning search

Naomi's knocking loudly on the door.
I'm still in my pajamas and come running
downstairs.

She's out of breath.
"After my dad left, Jax stayed outside.
I went up to bed and heard Mom and Dad
talking quietly at first, and then they got
louder and louder.
The door slammed after a bit.
I didn't think anything at the time.
The gate may have swung open.
When I looked in Jax's doghouse
this morning, it was empty."

I can tell Naomi's doing all
she can do not to cry. She's beside
herself. The trouble between us seems to
melt. No time for her to be mad at me.
She needs help. I'm glad she's here, and I'm
glad I'm here with her.
She has a picture in her hand, and she
wants to walk around and show the neighbors.

I quickly slide on shorts and grab flip-flops.
We walk behind backyards, calling for Jax.

Many dogs bark, but not him.
We are starting to hear a chorus of dogs
barking at each other way too early in the morning.

We take the picture to camp,
figure that the kids can be on the lookout
if they see him in the neighborhood.

Monday, July 10

The weekend passes and no Jax

Two days pass, and Naomi keeps
calling for Jax but is not looking
in the neighborhood.
She has given up.
She doesn't even go to practice.
Jerome said if she doesn't show up soon she might be
    benched.
She just sits there with her Tigers cap on
and tosses the ball from her hand to her
mitt, mitt to hand.

"You want to bike around and try again?"
"Nope."
Naomi heads back into the house.
I wait for a bit to see if she changes her mind.
Grandpa Herman comes out.
"She's just really upset," he says.

I am staring at the bowling ball.
"So you want to know why it's there?"
I nod.
"It's for my Isabelle. We were married
fifty-five years. It was her bowling ball.
She's buried at Rosehill Cemetery on Woodward.
I can't get there all the time,
hardly ever, but the bowling ball

was a part of us together, a happy and
healthy us.
Every time I see this
it helps me remember the good times."

I am getting choked up.
Wanting to know and knowing
are two different things,
like knowing that we moved so
Jerome might not go to Vietnam
and go to college instead.
We sit in our silence for a while,
and I thank him for the story.

Tuesday, July 11

What I hear

I skip camp today. I stop by to let Misty know.
I hop on my yellow banana-seat bike,
ride around to see if I can find Jax.

I go to the playground and then cross
Mt. Vernon Street to the other side of
the neighborhood where Daddy's work
friend is. I ride my bike, slowly pedaling my
feet, and ask if they've seen a black and white
dog. I show them pictures that we didn't post.
I'm about to turn around when I hear a faint bark,
a high-pitched painful type of yip that I
haven't heard before.

I think it's coming from the lot.
I stop at the edge of the field and listen again,
drop my bike to the side, look in all the spots
where Naomi and I play hide-and-seek.
I hear it again, and then I see him.
Jax has gotten himself caught
in a spring from that old couch.
He looks all worn out and pathetic.

At first I think I should hightail it back and let
Naomi know, but I don't want to leave him and
just want to get him out.

I know he wasn't here the last two days, since
we've been back and forth.

I approach slowly, not knowing about dogs,
but I've watched enough TV shows to know
that when animals get hurt,
they can act differently.

"Hey, Jax, it's okay. I'm gonna help you."
I walk over slowly, sit down on my haunches,
and have him sniff my hand. His deep brown eyes
recognize me, even though I barely get a tail wag.

I put out my hand, and he licks it slowly.
I can see a small thin wire wrapped around his back paw.
I try to twist it, but he yelps and looks scared.
I look around for something to bend the wire back
when I hear rustling in the bushes. I step behind the tree
to see who it is. It's that Joey.

He comes right up to Jax. He seems
quite comfortable with him.
"I'm sorry, buddy. How are we going to get
you out of this mess?" I watch him search through
his pocket and pull out a pocketknife.
"Wait!" I call out, not too loud to startle Jax.
"What are you going to do?"
I have never seen Joey like this.
He looks at me and says,
"How about you pull this wire up,
then gently bend the other? I'll cut
off this part, and then we can move it."

We are working together, and I can't believe he's not
being his usual mean self. I hold Jax's head to the side,
so he doesn't see what we are doing.
I hear a snap as Joey cuts through the metal.
Now we have a different problem.
We need to get the dog back to Naomi,
but he's too big to carry, and he's bleeding.

We both still have our bikes.
Joey looks up and says,
"You go ahead and get Naomi. I'll stay with the dog."
His eyes almost offer an apology.
I almost say that I should stay,
since the dog knows me better, but I'm a bit squeamish,
so I take off. I run through the thicket, fast as lightning.

I get to Naomi's house and start ringing the doorbell.
"Naomi, Naomi, we found Jax!"
She comes running out.
"Where's...Jax? What are you talking about?
"It's Jax! I found him in the field. He got caught
in the couch springs. We cut him loose,
but he's bleeding.
Get your grandpa to drive."
In a quick minute we are all in the car.
My heart is racing, and Naomi still looks
worried. I grab her hand.
"Who is *we*?"
"Joey and I—"
"Joey?"
"Yes, Joey."

We get to the field and Jax tries to get up

when he sees Naomi and Grandpa Herman.
Joey holds him down gently so he doesn't hurt
himself more.
We get the blanket out of the trunk and make
it into a stretcher. We place Jax in the back seat.
I tell them I'll walk back.
Joey looks up.
"You want to ride back together?"
"No thanks for the ride, but thank you
for helping."

Wednesday, July 12

A day for recovery

We both stay home from camp the next day.
I see Naomi on the porch.
"Jax got ten stitches, and he's got medicine to take.
Georgia, I can't believe that you and Joey—"
I stop her.
"Can I see Jax?"
We walk into the living room and he's sacked out,
snoring.

The sun's out

In the afternoon, Naomi's in the back.

Jax is on his blanket.

She's picking burrs out of his muddied coat.

Together we pick burrs.

We don't talk. We just pick burrs and flick them off.

"I want you to come with me to the awards ceremony
tomorrow...

I want you to know that I don't think you're second best."

Naomi takes her hat off, and her hair puffs out.

She pats me on the back, like I'm one

of the guys on her baseball team.

"Sure, I'll go. You're Jax's superhero, so why not?"

Admission

I decide to send a letter to Ty.
This is the kind of day that I would
tell him about.
He always looks after me.
Jerome treats me as if I'm
a bit like a yappy dog at his heels.

Dear Ty,

Sometimes strange things happen
and they get stranger.

This boy in the new neighborhood
has been my enemy.

We did a good thing together, even
though we may never be friends
since he's moving and he
has been a bully to me.
But just in a small moment,
it was okay.

I guess what I'm trying to
say is that sometimes
what is said is only a piece
of what is meant.

I'm so glad I could help
find Naomi's dog.

I wish you were close by.

I love you.

Georgia

Thursday, July 13

The ceremony

I go to camp as usual, knowing I am going
to the Spirit of Detroit Poetry Awards at Detroit Public
    Library.
I feel like Agent 99 in *Get Smart*. I'm wearing shorts,
but I've stuffed a nice dress and sandals in my
large beach bag. It's an odd feeling, knowing
that this is so important and I can't share it with
my family. One little lie and now it's getting bigger.

We go up to the Marathon station, just like Naomi
and I have done many times before. I need an additional
bus that goes up Woodward.
The ceremony is at two.
There are lots of men and women,
all dressed up with their kids.
Wanda's mom is there with Wanda and Ceci.
She motions for me to come join them.
Sitting at the end of the row is as close as I want to get.
Many important people are talking about
the Motor City and why it's so great!

"And, as you know, there are a lot
of young Detroiters here today waiting for the
winners of the Spirit of Detroit Poetry Contest.
The judges have had a hard time narrowing the entries
down,

so in an unprecedented move, we are going
to send the poems of the top two contestants back
to Miss Gwendolyn Brooks to pick the winning poem.
The winner will get an autographed
copy of her book and his or her poem painted on a wall
in Eastern Market.
Today I will be handing out
certificates to the two finalists.
Are there any questions?"
Dudley Randall, the poet, is reading the names.
He came to my school last year when we studied Miss
Brooks.
He said he and Gwendolyn Brooks were friends.
I wonder if he meant friends like Ceci and I are friends
or like Naomi and I are friends.

Suddenly, as if lightning could strike indoors,
Ceci's hand goes up, like it did all the time
in Mrs. Murphy's class, and she asks,
"Does the poet have to live in Detroit to win?"
"Well, this is a Detroit writing contest, isn't it?
And rules are rules."

I can barely look down the row. I can't believe
she is asking that. He reads two names from the list:
Charlie Cunningham and Georgia Johnson.
No Wanda Jarvis. We each go up to the podium and
get our certificate. Wanda gets an honorable mention.
This lie is getting bigger.

I read the certificate with my name.
There is a gold stamp on the edge of the paper.
I run my fingers over its raised edges.

I'd taken off my half-heart necklace when I got back
    from Detroit,
but I can see that Ceci still has hers on.
I plan on leaving without talking to any
of them. I will hold my head up and walk on out.
Ceci holds her hand out to congratulate me.
I am still holding my envelope
close to me, and I don't let go to shake Wanda
or Ceci's hand.

Needing permission

On the bus, I take the certificate out of the envelope.
There's something else inside. It's a note,
a permission slip, and an invitation
to city hall on Sunday, July 15.
Below the line it says that you must be accompanied
to city hall by an adult or family member over sixteen.
The signature form needs to be signed by a parent.
I hold it close and try not to have this ruin my feeling
good about being a finalist.

I get back, sneak up to my room, and have to find a new
hiding place. Jerome's shooting baskets,
not paying attention to me.
I place the envelope carefully in my closet cupboard and
slide the accordion door shut and begin to worry.

Knock on Jerome's door, up late

I stay up late, listening to
the radio, waiting until I hear
Jerome's door shut.

I knock a quiet knock and whisper,
"Jerome, open up. It's me, Georgia."
"G., what's going on and why aren't you asleep?"
"I've got a problem."
The whole story spills out.
He's looking at me like how did
I get into this mess?
I hand him the permission slip,
ask if he will sign it.

"G., this is on the date of the playoffs.
It says here the ceremony will be at ten Saturday morning.
That's the day of the Little League playoffs at two.
I can't, Georgia. That's way too close.
I don't think we can get back in time."

"Ty would do it!"
I can't believe the words that came from my mouth.
I don't know where that
came from, and I know it's a low blow.
I leave. I can't slam the door, even though I want to,
and go back to my room.

I pound on my pillow, take out my journal, and write.
I choose to write to my favorite brother.

Dear Ty,

I wish you were here.
By the time you get this, it won't
matter so much…
You'd help me in a minute…
I have good news.
I am a finalist
in the Spirit of Detroit Poetry Contest!
I need to bring someone
who's older than sixteen to sign
my permission slip to go to city hall
when they announce the final
prize winner.
I've asked Jerome.
He's not sure that he can go.
He has Little League playoffs.
I know that you would sign it.

Sorry.
Just having a hard time and
missing you.

Your Little Bit,

Georgia

While I am putting my letter
away, I hear footsteps coming
down the hall.
"G., where's the paper?
I'll sign it.
We'll figure it out
somehow."

Friday, July 14

How do we wear our lie?

At breakfast I feel as if
Mama and Daddy can see
that Jerome has agreed to come.
My guilt has grown, and I'm wearing
it like a dress of my mom's that I
can't fit into. It's drowning me.

Jerome's talking about the
playoffs this Saturday afternoon.
As he talks, all I can think about is the
contest.

He's telling them about the team's
standing and what the odds are to win.
Mama's beaming, looking so proud.

I wish that Mama could be that
proud of me being a finalist,
but this has gone on too long
and my lie won't permit it.

Friday, July 14 in the evening

Last game before the playoffs
tomorrow

The game starts at six. Jerome and Naomi go
early to practice. Their team's the Cardinals
and they're playing the Chicago White Sox.
Maybe this is a sign for the contest,
since Gwendolyn Brooks is from Chicago.

When we get to the field, I see
Naomi's mom, Grandpa Herman, Misty,
and her boyfriend.
We sit next to them.

There's only one set of bleachers,
so we are divided down the middle.
The teams are well-matched and it's
a tie at the third inning.

When Naomi puts on her batting
helmet, her hair pops out of the ponytail.
The kid next to me says, "Hey, how come that girl's
there? She can't play; she's not a boy."
Misty and I turn around at the same time
and tell him off.
"Shhh! She can do what she wants."

Naomi's up to bat and whales on the ball
and gets a double.
Next we hear some guy in the back
shouting, "That's the way, Naomi!"
I look at her grandpa Herman.
"Who's that?" I ask.
"That's her dad, finally coming
to watch his girl."

In the ninth inning, they break
the tie, which puts them in position
for the playoffs tomorrow.

Mama told me

I remember now the day that
Mama told me that we were moving.
Aunt Birdie and I were having brunch
with the birds at the Detroit Institute of Arts.
I was feeding the birds some crackers,
and they were fighting for the crumbs.
Aunt Birdie said that those two were going
after the snack like Jerome and I did
about every little thing.

When Mama told me, I was so upset.
I could barely look up at Diego Rivera's
mural on the way out, barely saw the
people he'd painted on the assembly lines.

It was before I knew there was a new house,
before I would meet a new friend who
liked baseball,
before Jerome would listen to my lie
and help me out,
before I knew he could be the type of
brother that Ty is for me.

Saturday, July 15

Today is the day

Jerome tells Mama and Daddy
that he's going to hang out
in Detroit with his friends
and he'll drop me off at Aunt Birdie's.
He's pretty good at this stretching-the-truth
thing too.

Going with Jerome is much
easier than going with Naomi.
Jerome has been going back and forth
to play ball and see his friends.
"Remember, we leave the library by twelve,
the game's at two and I have to get back.
Really, G., even if they have refreshments,
we gotta leave right after."

I hold the envelope close to me,
try to imagine the ceremony.
I am one of the final contestants.
I want to win, but if I don't, my lie
goes away.
But if I win, do I deserve to?

Before we go in,
I walk over to the bronze statue,
The Spirit of Detroit.

It's really a statue of a giant man sitting cross-legged.
In one hand, he holds a globe-shaped star,
in the other hand, a family.
It's the same statue that Ty and Jerome and I
sat on when Daddy took our picture for our family
card two Christmases ago.

The moment I've been waiting for...

We arrive at Detroit City Hall on Woodward.
We enter and show our tickets and permission
slips. The woman takes mine and shows us to
our seats.
Mr. Dudley Randall goes to the podium,
introduces himself and Reverend Nicholas Hood Sr.,
Detroit city councilman.
They will both be announcing the prize winner.

"Welcome to the Spirit of Detroit Poetry Contest.
These children are the future of our great city.
Their words—our words, words that we all need
to hear, need to echo in the theaters and resound
under the Windsor Tunnel to the sky above the
Ambassador Bridge."

And the winner is…

They've announced the third-place winner,
from the local Detroit library, and then the
second-place winner.
I haven't heard my name.
I'm really excited that I have a
chance; the other part of me has
that feeling in the pit of my stomach,
telling me that maybe I didn't win at all.

I shoot Jerome a sideways glance.
His eyebrows raise in a question mark,
and he shrugs his shoulders.

I want to place my
hands over my ears, disappear,
and then I hear:
"This year's winner is…Georgia Johnson
for her poem 'The Spirit of Detroit.'"
He reads the first three lines,
"It can shake, it can shimmy, it's a Motown sound."
My words being read by Dudley Randall,
the poet!

He asks me to come up and read my poem.
My throat dries up.
I didn't know that I would have to read.
I hadn't planned on this.

Jerome gives me kind
eyes, gives me a thumbs-up and mouths,
Read it for Ty.

I go up to the podium to receive my book.
I shake hands with Mr. Randall.
His eyes smile as he hands me the book,
Miss Gwendolyn Brooks's
Bronzeville Boys and Girls.

I lean down toward the mike, hope it doesn't
make that horrible squeaking noise, and begin to
read my poem.

Before I read my poem about shaking,
my knees are doing a pretty good job at that themselves.

The Spirit of Detroit

It can shake,
it can shimmy,
it's a Motown sound.
R-E-S-P-E-C-T, Aretha,
it's time to go downtown...
to the heat of summer
with hydrants on.

To the river,
across from Windsor,
on the Fourth of July night,
fireworks late,
Astoria Bridge lights,
neon signs flashing on Woodward
and drag racing fights.

Sewer grates steaming like dragons.
J.L. Hudson's department store,
the smell of clean linens.

Eastern Market veggies and eggs,
chickens strut around.
Fisher Building skyscraper,
gold and greenish brown.

The Spirit of Detroit statue
sits in front of city hall,
holding the sphere of the
city's families, holding us all.

It's all done

I hear the audience clap
and feel a bit dizzy.
I clutch the handrail
with one hand and carefully
hold my book.
My face feels warm.
I sit down, open the book, and trace
Miss Gwendolyn Brooks's signature
on the dedication page.

Jerome gives me a quick hug
and reminds me—we're in a hurry,
no time to go to the reception.
We need to go…

The return trip

We are back on the bus.
My stomach feels funny.
I can smell the book,
the ink,
the paper,
and now the bus fumes.

I don't feel right.
I begin to feel dizzy
with the excitement of
the day, the heat of July.

We've been on the bus
for a few minutes, and I look
at the autograph of Miss Brooks.
She has signed it:
To Georgia, keep on writing.
I feel like this book is not mine to keep,
like I'm an imposter.
I remember her poem "Truth."
My Detroit, my familiar,
is now not mine?

I close the book and tell Jerome,
"We need to go back—"
"Georgia, come on! We just left.
The playoffs start at two."
He knows I won't stop.
I pull the cord, and the bell rings

for the bus to stop.
"Georgia, come on…don't…"
But I already have one foot out the door.
Jerome follows me reluctantly but quickly.

We cross the street to the other
side of Woodward and wait for the
southbound bus.
Jerome's so mad he can barely talk.
"I have to give this book back," I tell him.

Contest imposter

We are back at city hall.
Jerome won't even come in, he's so steamed.
He's pacing back and forth, and I run back in
with the book.
The auditorium's empty.
I start to panic because no one's nearby.
Then I remember the reception.
I return to the lobby and look for the room number
on the glass board.

Reception: Room 117.
There are still a few people there.
My eyes dart around the room.
I try to be quick.
I find the city councilman and the poet.
They reach out to shake my hand again,
ask if they can take another quick picture.

The lie unravels so fast.

"I need to tell you something. It's important.
I've moved. I no longer live in Detroit."
There is a long silence, a very long silence,
and then the two men start to whisper back and forth.
"We need to go talk to the final judge."
I see them conferring.
Jerome is tapping, pacing back and forth
and mumbling, "Georgia…"

They return and look serious
and begin to ask questions.
"Were you born in Detroit?"
"Yes."
"Did you write this poem when
you lived in Detroit?"
"Yes."
"Georgia Johnson, you are a Detroit girl.
Your spirit and heart are here, no matter
where you go."

I start to breathe again,
thank them and leave quickly,
knowing that Jerome's probably
not speaking to me now, and I
don't blame him.

The quiet ride back

There is no conversation
on the bus ride home.

I apologize, don't know what more to say,
so I don't.

When we get back, Mama wants to know
why we cut it so close.
"Naomi's already come by to gather equipment."

Jerome runs to the garage and gets
his gear and rushes out.
Luckily, Mama doesn't have time
to ask any questions since we
are going to the playoffs.

"Why are you dressed so nice?"
"Just wanted to show Aunt Birdie this dress, Mama."

I hide the book behind my back and run upstairs,
place it under my pillow, get shorts on, and
go to the playoffs…some lies gone,
but others are still here.

I'm going to tell Mama.

Victory

Jerome's kids are ready when we arrive.
They are in their starting lineup, even though
they will bat second.

The director of the Park District
makes announcements and encourages
everyone to play fair and have a good time.

We stand up for "The Star-Spangled Banner."
My mama and daddy
take this very seriously, even for
Little League, out of respect for Uncle Russell
and Ty.
Daddy takes his hat off, and Mama places
her hand to her heart and I do the same.

The game is fairly even in all innings,
but Jerome's team is tied at the bottom of the eighth
and, luckily, has the last ups.

Daddy sees the batting order and thinks
Jerome has a good plan. Naomi's a hitter.
He has her placed fifth. There's a kid on
second, and Joey's on third base at the bottom of the
      ninth.
Naomi's up. She knocks it clear to the
grassy part of the playground. Her triple
breaks the tie, and victory is theirs.

The Good Humor truck in the parking lot

Jerome promised to buy all the kids
ice cream if they won or not.
They all gather around, carry Naomi
up high in the air, and celebrate.

Parents come up to Jerome and my folks;
they want to thank him for coaching, want to know
if he will be coaching next summer.

"If I'm here, I will."
I notice Mama looks worried,
but tonight's a night for celebrating,
for many reasons, even for something that
Mama doesn't know about.

But now is Jerome's limelight,
and when we walk back to the house,
I grab his hand and say thank you,
nuzzle my head into his shoulder and say,
"Please don't join the Army..."
"I'm proud of you, Georgia, and where
else can I find someone who bothers me so much?"
We hug.

When we get back

When we get back, Daddy wants
to take another picture with his Polaroid
camera.
He takes one of Jerome and Naomi
with their uniforms on,
then one of all of us without him,
and then asks Grandpa Herman to take
one of the four of us.

It takes a while for the image to show up.
It always seems like magic when
the people appear, and it always smells
like a strong chemical from the hairdressers.

"G., if you want to send anything to Ty, give
it to me tomorrow and I'll mail it on Monday."
I give him a big hug.
I know exactly what I will
send, and I run upstairs
and begin copying my poem as
Jerome showers after his victory.

The day after

I wake up,
wonder if the contest
was a dream.

I feel the book
beneath my pillow—
the book, my book,
Gwendolyn Brooks's poems,
now mine.

The sun creeps
into the space
between the shade and curtain.

There's just enough light to see
Miss Brooks's autograph.
I smell the book, inhale
the sweet odor of ink
on paper.

So much good yesterday…
Me winning,
Jerome's team winning,
me lying and winning,
me telling the truth and winning.
I told the truth to the

whole city of Detroit, but still not yet
to Mama.

I never keep secrets from Mama.

Looking for...

Naomi and I are going to hang out today,
play board games and feel good about
winning,
maybe go up to 10 Mile and Evergreen
and Baskin-Robbins.

Even though the house is new, I still don't like
being in basements alone.
"Mama, come down to the basement with me."
"Georgia, I've got a lot to do to prepare for class
tomorrow. Maybe this afternoon."

I am in search of the box labeled *Games*.
I've promised Naomi a Monopoly challenge.
I'm sure she'll win. She's so competitive.

We don't have an attic that you can
go up into like in Detroit,
where there's a closet called a cedar
closet. I pull the cord for the light.

Mostly, there are boxes
that might never be unpacked.
Mama has many boxes down here
labeled *Lecture Notes* and *Daddy's Plans*.
One box is marked *School*.
I open it, see that Mama has kept
our school pictures for each year.
I take one of Ty's graduation

pictures and place it in my pocket,
look through Jerome's Little League
pictures, my school photo from sixth grade.
Ceci's right in front of me since she's shorter.
She still is and I'm still tall.
I see the box of games. Scrabble's
first—that's Ty's and my favorite.
Monopoly's below, not my favorite
since Jerome always beats me, and
with Naomi it will be the same.
I see a box marked *Ty*.
I take the tape off carefully
so I can replace it.
It's his Boy Scout box.
I find his sash with his sewn-on badges.
There are several craft projects, a leather knife case,
a belt buckle. I see something wrapped up.
It's fairly light. I unwrap layers of tissue.
It's a small wooden birdhouse.
I look at the bottom:
Ty Johnson 1960 Troop # 542
I bring it upstairs and leave the
games behind.

Mama's in the kitchen.
I hold the birdhouse behind my back,
not sure if Mama wants it
unpacked, but I know I want to
hang it outside on our tree.
"Georgia?"
"Mama, can I put this—?"
Before I can finish, Mama
barely gets out a "Sure."

She starts to cry and holds me close.
I take Mama's hand, and we
walk out together and place it
on a sturdy branch.

Mama and I sit there awhile,
and she starts to sing.
"Hush, little baby, don't say
a word, Mama's gonna buy
you a mockingbird. And if that
mockingbird don't sing—"
I chime in, "Mama's gonna
buy you a diamond ring."
My bedtime song for a very
long time.

It's quiet for a bit,
and then we hear the sound
of the moving truck and look up.
We hear the squeaks of the brakes
and look down the street.
It looks like moving day for
Joey.

Mama and I sit in a loud silence.
We know what it's like to leave
and to stay.

When the truck pulls
past the house, Joey looks
and sends a small wave.

We sit on the step for what
seems like a long-short time.

I need to do one more thing
before I can tell Mama.

Supplies

At night, I call Aunt Birdie,
ask her if we can go to the hardware
store when Naomi and I get there tomorrow.

Naomi's made a list of things that
we need for the wall—large sponges,
sandpaper, primer, three gallons of paint,
and a ladder.

Naomi has helped her daddy
paint after the drywall is hung
in the new houses in our neighborhood
and is pretty handy.

Aunt Birdie says yes but wants to know why.
I tell her that it's a surprise and that
she will find out tomorrow.

Mama still doesn't know

This time when Mama drops
us off, she won't know how
many times we have been
here this summer, taken off
on our own,
doesn't know that we know the
bus route back and forth
from Southfield to Detroit.

She doesn't know that I need
to leave a piece of me there,
doesn't know that I did this for
Ty and me,
doesn't know that my words
need to stay here,
to say that Georgia was here.

Ty doesn't know how many miles
from Motown our new house really is.
I will leave my words on the alley wall
next to Aunt Birdie's house,
behind Mr. Weiss's Deli,
like a street sign or a billboard
that reads *Home.*

Together again

Mama drops us off. We go into
Aunt Birdie's house, and I know
now is the time to tell her, to come clean.

I tell Aunt Birdie about the contest,
the address, my lie, the bad news,
the contest, and my good news.

Aunt Birdie listens, her eyebrows
raised up.
"That's not the Georgia that I know.
I thought I saw that rust-stained heart
on my mailbox.
I thought something was up."

I wait for a scolding from Aunt Birdie,
but instead she comes up and gives me a big
hug. "So what are we waiting for? Let's go
to the hardware store."
We walk around the back alley, weeds tall
as they scratch my legs, yellow moth butterflies
fluttering up as we walk.
I lift up the garage handle, and we
both push and move around to the side door,
get in the car, and drive down Livernois
to Jack's Hardware on Woodward.

The mural

When we return, I see a crew
I wasn't expecting—Ceci, her mama and papa,
and the boys. Ceci's there without Wanda.

"What? No Wanda?"
I don't know what got into me,
but I guess I'm still a little mad.
She tells me, "I got tired of her
after a few weeks. She was too
agreeable. She got on my nerves.
She just agreed all the time.
I got bored. I like how you
have some zing to you!"

We prime the walls, let them dry in the
midmorning summer sun.
For the next coat, we blend perfect blues for
a perfect sky.

In the afternoon, we take out Aunt Birdie's
special chalk-like pencils to draw the outlines,
and I write my poem on the wall.
Everyone else draws in the details of Detroit—
records and music notes for Motown,
Stroh's ice cream cones and bottles of beer,
Eastern Market with a picture of the chicken's
head at the entrance, and sketches of cars
to show the Motor City.

Now we can come back and forth this summer
to finish painting this wall.
Mama can drive us on her way
to work without the secrets.

I pick up the pencil and write
in the far right-hand corner,
in my very best cursive,
Georgia was here
because I was and always will be.

The truth

I hear the car door slam
and the squeak of the
screen of the front door,
and I know Mama's here.

Aunt Birdie goes back inside,
and Mama comes out with her.
I grab Mama's hand and lead the way.

This is my way, for now, of telling her a part
of my lie, these words, my words,
my need to win the contest,
to tell her the truth
and tell her my lie.
I want to show her that I was right and wrong,
which all seems smaller now,
but now, in this moment, we are here,
back in Detroit.

I show her my Gwendolyn Brooks book,
point to my words on the wall,
hold her hand in mine,
and trace the title,
The Spirit of Detroit.
I begin to read her my poem.
It can shake it can shimmy,
it's a Motown sound.

Mama leans over
and plants a kiss on top of my head
to add to my kiss tree.

Now I know
my new home
is only miles from here,
like an inch on a map,
which seems so much smaller now.

Acknowledgements

Many thanks to Jaynie Royal, Publisher and Editor-in-Chief of Regal House Publishing, and to Pam Van Dyk, Managing Editor, for awarding *Miles from Motown* Finalist in the Kraken Contest for MG manuscripts in 2019. Without this recognition, this book would not have happened. Gratitude to Pam Van Dyk, my editor, who had a keen sense for the story and the time period, which enabled her to relate so intuitively to the story.

Thanks to the many people who have helped and supported the writing of this work, including Juliet Bond, Margo Rabb, Sarah Aronson, and SCBWI-IL for all of the opportunities, critiques and support which grew my confidence as a writer and respectful storyteller. I would like to thank Principal Sylvie Anglin for facilitating many grants from the University of Chicago Laboratory Schools' professional development fund so that I could participate in transformational writer's workshops.

Thank you to The Highlights Foundation for providing phenomenal workshops with remarkable authors, writers, and community for aspiring and established writers. An abundance of gratitude to Ellen Pridmore and Megan Kelly, critique partners, who believed in this story, and saw it through many revisions; to J.S.Puller for early and insightful feedback; to critique partner, Carol Coven Grannick, for an exchange of our novels-in-verse which brought us both closer to publication; and to Libby Ester and Lisa Maggiore, who were always available for all "post-production" detail work.

There are not sufficient words to convey what Esther Hershenhorn does for writers in the SCBWI community. As my writing coach, she was supportive, creative, and the most positive advocate I could have had always seeing new possibilities. Thank you, Esther, for putting up with my detours and tangents, and bringing my focus back to the story when I strayed.

Thank you to my family with love to Deb Frankenberry, Deborah Sukenic, Silvia Sukenic, and Lili Sukenic for being a first reader and editor.